THE SUNSHINE CRUST BAKING FACTORY

BY STACY WAKEFIELD

Published by Akashic Books
©2014 Stacy Wakefield
ISBN-13: 978-1-61775-303-9
Library of Congress Control Number: 2014955088

The first two chapters of this novel appeared in an earlier form in *Narrative* (narrativemagazine.com) in May 2011.

Akashic Books
Twitter: @AkashicBooks
Facebook: AkashicBooks
E-mail: info@akashicbooks.com
Website: www.akashicbooks.com

For Kyanne and Letha

New York City, July 1995

I

When I showed up in New York with my dog-eared copy of *Hopping Freight Trains* and my new tattoo, I thought getting a room at a squat would be a cinch. These were my people, right?

My dad had been worried by the tattoo. He'd asked if it might make it harder for me to find a job. But that was the whole point. People spent all their time working stupid jobs so they could buy a bunch of crap they didn't need. The whole routine was for suckers. I wouldn't need money when I was a squatter, and to join the squatters, I had to mark myself as rejecting mainstream society and its ass-backward priorities. The tattoo was a better investment than college. I could have convinced him if his new wife hadn't been looking over his shoulder making that face.

Anyway, it turned out getting into a squat was harder than joining a sorority: hopeless. I went to every show, every workday, every Food Not Bombs and

Critical Mass, but the squats were all full. I'd had some vague idea about squatting my own building, but my older friend Donny, who was like my squatting mentor, said I'd never find an empty building on the Lower East Side now—I was ten years too late. He said to check out Brooklyn. But who wanted to go to Brooklyn? I didn't come all the way to New York City to live out in the middle of nowhere.

Then I met Lorenzo.

He was sleeping on the roof of ABC No Rio like me and a bunch of other summer campers and transients. It was tent city up there. I'd seen him around and knew who he was. I had his band's first seven-inch and I'd even interviewed the singer for the zine I did in high school. That was just a few months before they'd broken up after a fight so spectacular it resulted in a fire and ten arrests at a squat in Berlin on the last show of their tour. Everyone knew the story; they were notorious.

One night he was sitting near the edge of the roof drinking a forty and I went and said hi and we got to talking. It was too hot to sleep; the air was thick and oily. Lorenzo told me about the music scene in Mexico City where he grew up, about the squats his band played at in Europe, and how he'd come to New York to start a new band. He wanted to squat a building too, so I told him what Donny had said about Brooklyn, about all the empty buildings out there. I repeated what Donny had told me, that a new building had been squatted just this year in an area called Williamsburg. I liked sounding like I knew a thing or two about New York already. Lorenzo had this amused look, like life was a big messy show put on for his entertainment. The way he told stories about cops attacking a squat he was staying at in Bologna or getting strip-searched by border guards in Switzerland or hitchhiking through Spain—it seemed like he never took anything too seriously. He made me want to go on adventures with him. And okay, he was seriously good-looking. He had dark eyes and a sly smile and a Crass tattoo. I was flattered by how he took for granted that I knew the bands and cities he mentioned, talking low so all the people sleeping around us couldn't hear.

Lorenzo was into it and suddenly being out in Brooklyn didn't sound so bad. He said it'd be so much better to start a building ourselves and invite in who we wanted, instead of kissing ass at the established squats. He said a German dude had told him how to figure out if a building was abandoned: you hide a matchstick in the doorframe, and if it's still there a week later you know no one is going in or out. He knew all kinds of tricks like that. I got my map out of my bag. Williamsburg was right over the river. It was the new frontier. We agreed to go explore after dark one night. I could hardly believe my luck. Lorenzo from Disguerro! He was so cool! We were going to be a team!

I didn't see him the next day. When night fell, I went up and sat on the roof to wait for him. The later it got, the more I worried. Maybe I'd misunderstood.

Maybe he meant another day. Then it was midnight and I started thinking I'd gotten carried away. Probably he was just talking. Why would a guy like Lorenzo move all the way out to Brooklyn? Maybe he'd gotten offered another place to live. Or even worse: maybe he could see I liked him even though I'd tried to be cool and it scared him off. That had happened before. Guys think I'm great because I'm not girly, we like the same bands and talk about records, and they *really* like me, but when it comes down to it, they can't deal with the size of my ass. He'd probably hooked up with one of these skinny waitresses with a Betty Page haircut and tattoos. They were all over the neighborhood and they had apartments with air-conditioning. Lorenzo was probably somewhere like that right now, watching cable TV. He looked like a glue-sniffing badass from Mexico City, but he'd let some things slip last night—like how his sister did ballet . . . I stopped myself. He was gone one night and I was turning on him like a crazy person. Take a breath, Sid, I told myself. Go to bed.

The next day I distracted myself by drawing in my sketchbook. I only worked one day a week, running Donny's record and zine table at hardcore matinees at ABC No Rio, so I didn't have anything I had to do. I drew Mohawked punks getting chased by cops. Riot grrrls beating perverts with their little purses. Yuppies being devoured by their designer furniture. When I was immersed in a drawing I forgot about everything else— like the fact that summer was going to be over soon and if I didn't find someplace to live I was going to have to take a bus back to New England and beg my old boss to give me my stupid job at the comic store back.

Then, on the third night, Lorenzo showed up after midnight. He whispered, "C'mon," and I jumped out of my sleeping bag and laced up my boots.

Delancey Street was just one block south of ABC No Rio. And there it was: the Williamsburg Bridge. I'd never thought about where it went. Squatters never left the Lower East Side, never took the subway. Everyone bragged about how many years it had been since they'd gone above 14th Street. The bridge rose huge and monstrous with a wide iron staircase right in the middle, traffic sweeping around on both sides.

We climbed up the stairs and the walkway twisted and turned and got really narrow. I was hyper-alert but Lorenzo seemed relaxed, humming a bass line under his breath. He wasn't a big guy, he was just a little taller than me, compact and scrappy, with black dreadlocks that grew forward over his face. Above the river the walkway widened.

"What's that one?" Lorenzo pointed up the East River.

"Queensboro Bridge."

We were up high enough now to see past the projects and tenements on the East River to the lights of Midtown. The Empire State Building was lit red, white, and blue for the Fourth of July. I bit my tongue to keep from pointing it out, afraid I'd sound like a tour guide. I was so relieved Lorenzo was back, I had to watch it or I'd gush.

Across the water, the Domino Sugar factory smoldered on the river, smelling like burnt toast. The rest of Williamsburg was in shadow. Low buildings, dark. We climbed down rickety caged stairs under a dripping highway overpass and now we were in Brooklyn, with none of the fanfare of the Manhattan side. Donny had said Williamsburg had once been a thriving industrial area but now most of the factories facing the bridge were boarded up and derelict.

Lorenzo walked back toward the water, staying close to the bridge. A mangy dog with no collar passed, head low, eyes tilted up suspiciously.

We turned north on a street near the water and found ourselves drawn to a narrow brick building. It rose out of an overgrown lot like a weed, on a little street that sloped down to the Domino factory. The windows on the first floor were bricked over and upstairs they were covered in plywood. It was very exposed and alone in its little yard, but its small scale was appealing.

When we got closer we could see the spray-painted square above the front door, with one line across it. Donny said a square with an X meant the fire department had cut holes in the roof to ventilate in case of fire. A square with no X meant they hadn't cut it open yet—that was the symbol to look for. But one line? What did that mean?

We climbed a weedy cement stoop to the front door. It was padlocked from the outside but the wood was so old Lorenzo was able to slip his Leatherman under the screws and pry the whole thing off the frame while I watched for cars. There was no one around.

Lorenzo pushed inside and then stood holding onto the doorframe with his sinewy arm. I looked over his shoulder. My tiny Maglite illuminated the threshold and then, past that, no floor at all. We were standing above a black pit of rubble. A little streetlight filtered down through the loose boards over the windows and our eyes slowly adjusted. Above us, what must have once been three stories had collapsed into the basement.

"It's like being inside a chimney." My whisper echoed through the tall space.

We explored the neighborhood until dawn, and then the next night, and the next. There were blocks tight with shabby vinyl-sided row houses, bicycles and cats outside. Low concrete warehouses with metal roll gates that were probably in use during the day. There were plenty of boarded-up buildings, but they were all too huge, too well-sealed, too close to inhabited buildings.

I kept notes of addresses to watch in my sketchbook. I wasn't sure we were getting anywhere but I liked hanging out with Lorenzo. I felt cool just walking next to him. We fit together so well, we walked at the same pace, and we had so much in common. We'd both given up trying to be vegan, we both thought the Ramones were overrated and secretly loved Guns N' Roses, we both had Infest and Born Against patches on our backpacks. The difference was, Lorenzo actually knew those guys. He'd met and played with all my favorite bands, he'd stayed at their houses and borrowed their gear. And now he was here with me.

We kept going back to the building we called the Chimney to check on our matchstick, and it hadn't budged. One night while we stood outside, Lorenzo gave me a sly look, his dark eyes shadowed by long lashes. He said we should spend the night inside. I was game. Really, when he looked at me like that, I was game for anything.

I held my flashlight in the doorway while Lorenzo got the door open. We let our eyes adjust standing on the edge of the stoop by the door, then he maneuvered around the rubble pit to the bigger ledge in back, nimble as a rock climber.

I held tight to the wall, finding footholds in the brick. It reminded me of the abandoned railroad bridge where the kids from my high school hung out drinking beer. I was the one who couldn't wait to climb to the top first. Which made the boys mad because then they had to climb as high as me. It was easier for them, they didn't have boobs getting in the way. From the platform near the ground, the girls would cry at us not to go too high, missing all the fun. This ledge might not be high up but it was narrow and I was slow and awkward. I'm not big because I'm a lazy slob, like everyone thinks fat people are. It's just how I'm built, there's nothing I can do about it.

Lorenzo held out his hand from the platform in back and I took it even though I didn't need help. His grip was warm and tight and made my head feel like it was going to explode. Luckily it was too dark for him to see me blush. A scurrying sound in the pit made us flinch. Lorenzo let go of my hand and sat against the wall. The platform was like a deck over a lake. He pulled his knees up to his chin so skin was visible through the holes in his Carhartts.

"We get boards, we can stretch them across," he said, pointing, "put in a new floor."

I eased down next to him. It smelled foul. Where would we get boards that long, and how would we get them into the building unseen? How much would they cost? I wondered if the squat Donny had told us about was close by. They must have had to do these things too. I wished we could ask them how.

I pulled the sketchbook out of my backpack, stretched out with the big flashlight next to me, and drew a floor plan of the space, so we could organize materials later. I marked where the windows were and the front door. The scurrying came and went. The night was hot, the air in the building thick and stagnant, but I pulled my hoodie around me to cover my skin. I shut my eyes for a moment.

A sound startled me, shrieking from the pit. I jerked up, my back stiff.

"What happened?" Lorenzo growled, all groggy. He'd dozed off.

"My pencil," I said. It had rolled into the pit. I didn't want to fall asleep again. Next it would be *me* rolling in there.

We left to get some air, plodding through the neighborhood, all sweaty, not talking. I tied my hoodie around my waist and sipped from my water bottle, wishing I had gum to kill the dead taste in my mouth. We crossed a highway overpass above the Brooklyn-Queens Expressway. Thin, late-night traffic flowed below us, a few trucks. On the other side Lorenzo flicked my arm and stopped short. I froze. He was looking at a man framed in a circle of lamplight a block away.

We eased back, staying behind a short fence around a little playground. The man was wearing a sweatshirt with the hood up despite the heat. He had a flashlight gripped in his teeth and he was crouched at the lamppost with tools.

From around a corner a dog appeared. She paused, paw up, alert. The man was intent on what he was doing, he didn't see the dog or us. The dog walked toward him, head down. From the corner two more dogs appeared behind her, then another, even more starved and skinny, with a limp. They approached the man with surprising speed.

Lorenzo moved in a flash. The man looked up and saw him and fell back from his crouch, catching himself hard on one wrist. The flashlight hit the pavement. The dog was on the man already, jaws aimed at his hand on the ground. Lorenzo's boot connected with her side and she skittered away, snarling. Lorenzo made a guttural cry and lunged and she backed off. Her pack scattered behind her. They turned tail and fled the way they had come.

I jogged up to the lamppost, my heart racing. The man was on his feet now. He looked like an athlete under his hood and he was young. He was wearing work gloves.

He stared at Lorenzo and me like he was trying to place us as well—our army backpacks, boots, my bangs under a bandanna. I don't know what we looked like we might be doing in the neighborhood at this time of night. We stood there together, breathing hard, taking each other in while traffic continued below us on the BQE. On one side, a residential street of tight row houses covered in vinyl and fake brick hummed with air conditioners and sleeping people.

A door slammed and our three heads spun to watch a short guy burst out of the brick building nearest us. He had a nervous look and straight hair pulled back in a ponytail. He was wearing beat-up dress shoes and acid-washed jeans.

"You okay?" he asked the big guy, uncertainly.

The big guy nodded. "Those damn dogs. And I thought this guy was about to mug me. But he was just quicker on the take than me. Thanks, man." He reached to shake Lorenzo's hand.

"Was it that yellow dog?" The little guy hugged his arms tight to his chest. "That dog's mean, I see him around all the time."

"Yeah, yellow," Lorenzo said.

I looked back at the dark building. From a third-story window, a cord snaked over the road and dangled down loose next to the lamppost. The tall guy followed my eyes. On the sidewalk were clippers, screwdriver, wire nuts. He wasn't tagging; he was hooking up electricity. From the lamppost. When I put that together, I almost yelled out loud. This must be the squat Donny had told us about! Lorenzo and I caught each other's eyes. These guys wouldn't be intimidated by getting thirty-foot lumber into their building. These were the people to know.

We stayed with the big guy, Mitch, while the nervous long-haired one, Skip, ran back up to the fuse box on the third floor. I held my big flashlight and Lorenzo gripped a wire with his Leatherman while Mitch connected it. When Mitch stood, looking up at the window expectantly, my heart was in my throat with excitement.

Skip's head darted out of an upstairs window and he whistled. Mitch led us into the building. The air inside the cramped foyer was cooler and damper than outside. Rubble crunched under our feet. Mitch ducked his head beneath a beam held at a wacky angle by two metal columns, and went up a narrow staircase.

At the top of the stairs was a room as wide as the building and circled with windows. Real windows with glass in them. The front of the building faced the residential street, looking out toward apartments. To the west was the highway. We crossed a clean, even wood-plank floor to where Skip bent over an outlet on the wall and a shadeless lamp. He plugged it in. Nothing happened. Skip squatted down and we hovered, breath held. He felt for the switch and with a click, the bare bulb glowed. Skip looked up at us all, his mouth open with surprise and pleasure, the underglow giving him a carnival effect.

"Touchdown!" Mitch crowed, and gave Lorenzo a high five.

We flopped down in a circle around the lamp like it was a campfire. Skip scurried into a dark room somewhere and was back with two beers dangling from a six-pack string. He flipped them both open and gave one to Mitch and one to Lorenzo. They drank and handed the cans to Skip and me. The beer was warm and flat. My eyes roamed over the big room. The ceiling was low but soundly finished with old acoustic tiles.

Lorenzo asked how long they'd been there.

Mitch had taken off his hoodie. Underneath he had on a worn Red Sox T-shirt. He had very light, very short hair and pale skin and bruised-looking eyes. He looked like a marine, muscular and square. He said he'd been there since April without electricity; a guy at work had just told him how to hook it up. He spoke in the first person like he lived there alone and Skip watched and looked nervous and said nothing. I wanted to ask a million more questions—where he worked, what had happened since April, who else lived here—but I didn't want to sound like an undercover cop.

"We're working on a building over on Wythe Avenue," I told them.

Lorenzo scoffed. "It's fucked up, though. We can't never get that shit together for winter. It's not like this place."

"We've been staying at ABC No Rio," I explained. They looked at me blankly. "It's a squat on the Lower East Side . . . you know? They, like, have events and stuff . . ."

"I just moved here," Mitch shrugged.

"What kind of events?" Skip asked.

"Like, a concert-hall kind of space. Punk bands and anti-folk, um . . . art, Wednesday's poetry . . ."

"Open mic?" Skip's mouth curved into a smile. "I thought you might be a writer."

Actually, I went to the hardcore shows on the weekends and made fun of the poetry nerds, but I didn't say that.

Mitch tipped back his beer can, taking a long drink. "Well, if you guys need a place, check out the first floor. No one's using it."

"Really? Are you serious?" I looked from him to Skip and then to Lorenzo. A whole floor? Just like that? Didn't they need to discuss it amongst themselves?

Skip watched me like he wasn't surprised by Mitch's invitation, only curious to see what we'd say.

Lorenzo raised his can and said, "Cheers to that, man."

Mitch raised his can to tap Lorenzo's and the shadows of their hands flickered up the wall.

II

One summer I'd worked for a company that cleaned houses after someone died in them. I thought about that in the hardware store in Brooklyn the next day, deciding what I needed to get started on that first floor. Bleach, garbage bags, work gloves. That blew twenty dollars right there. Shit. Luckily, I was working for Donny on Sunday. He paid me forty dollars for the afternoon. All summer I'd managed to live off that.

The guy who opened the door at the squat wasn't Mitch or Skip but a clean-cut Latino with short hair and a thin mustache. He was wearing a wifebeater and eating a piece of celery.

"I'm Sid," I introduced myself. "Your housemate said—"

"I gotta say," his voice was higher than I expected, "I did *not* believe it." He leaned against the door frame. "That's something. A girl in a place like this!" He laughed like that was a great joke. "Eddie." He reached out a hand. "Steady Eddie, six months clean and counting."

Oh, great. AA. I knew too much about that from my mom.

"So you and your man gonna have a go at this first

floor, huh?" He gestured at a black maw on the far side of the foyer. There was no door but the sunlight didn't penetrate far inside. "I never even been in there."

The building had once been a commercial bakery and the ovens had been down here. I stepped into the dark. There had been a fire and the space was destroyed. My eyes adjusted slowly and I saw a tiny window in back. One window. Through the piles of junk, rubble, old burnt wooden beams, trash, crap.

"Shit, I don't know." Eddie let out a whistle, holding his nose. "This is, like, toxic and shit. You got kids?"

"Kids?" Jesus, how old did he think I was? "No!"

"That's cool," he nodded at me with big sincere eyes, "I hear your man saved Mitch from some rabid dog, right?"

I started to tell him Lorenzo and I were just friends, but he put up his hands in defense, like I'd told him to mind his own business. "Oh shit, you don't got to tell me!" He went back upstairs.

I had my whole box of garbage bags used up in a couple hours. The rubble and metal pieces were so heavy I could only put a few things in each bag, but I had to start somewhere. I looked up when a shadow blocked the light from the door. I recognized the powerful shoulders even before I could see his face.

"Hey, Mitch!" I rubbed my face, smearing black soot around.

He was holding one of the garbage bags I'd put outside and he dropped it with a thud. "You put this stuff on the curb?" I couldn't see his face in the shadow. "You think the city picks up our garbage?" I hadn't noticed how strong his Boston accent was last night.

"Sorry." I jumped up. "What should I do with it?"

Mitch was already heading up the stairs, one arm resting on the beam just over his head, one red-and-black high-top Air Jordan tapping on the next step. "I don't know, go to the dump or whatever."

"Dump? Where's the—"

"You know what?" He continued up, shaking the brown bag in his hand at me. "I just got off work. I got a date with a pastrami sandwich."

I stood in the doorway, listening to the floorboards creak on the second floor as he walked over my head. Then up the next stairway, then silence. I looked out at the curb at my pile of heavy bags. I brought them all back in, and then sat on a milk crate outside the door trying to cool off, totally defeated, hoping Lorenzo would show up already. Maybe he was practicing with his new band today. That's what he had come to New York for, not to muck around in this filth. Who could blame him.

I was starving, out of water. But I couldn't leave. I didn't have a key, someone had to lock the door behind me. I lingered a little longer, hoping Mitch would come back down. Maybe he'd apologize for being so brusque, help me figure out what to do.

Finally, I tiptoed upstairs feeling like a kid going to the principal's office. I crossed the second floor where the lamp we'd turned on last night still sat by the wall. There was another staircase and I climbed up higher. The third floor was even nicer than the second. It was a huge open space with a high ceiling and columns and tall windows that let a breeze through. Way in the back was a doorway, and I heard a radio playing Pearl Jam.

I called, "Mitch?" but there was no answer. I made myself march to the open doorway. Mitch was lying on his bed with his shirt off and his eyes closed, one arm wrapped around a pillow behind his head. The skin of his chest was so pale it was almost translucent. When I knocked on the doorframe he opened his eyes slowly, unsurprised, like he knew I was there.

"Can you lock me out? I gotta . . . uh . . . go out . . ." The tremor in my voice was pathetic.

I went to ABC No Rio and saw that Lorenzo's sleeping bag and backpack were gone. I went through my stuff and found two novels I'd borrowed from Raven, a girl I'd met at Food Not Bombs. I figured I'd go return them; I loved talking to Raven, she'd cheer me up. No matter what came up, she had a position on it. When I got blisters from wearing Chuck Taylors with no socks, she said I should pee on my foot every morning to stave off infection. That cracked me up.

Not very many people lived at ABC No Rio, and those who did were older and almost normal-looking. But you could tell Rot-Squat was a punk house from a block away. A narrow-eyed guy in a spiked vest and newsboy cap was on the stoop drinking from a grimy Gatorade bottle. I knew him, his name was Stumps. He was like a doorman, with keys and dog tags around his neck. He let me pass and I climbed up the crooked stairs that looked like they'd been built by the Little Rascals.

Raven wasn't in her room on the second floor so I kept going. Her crew hung out upstairs a lot. When I knocked on Lee and Jessica's open door, it was Raven's head—shaved except for three long dreadlocks sprouting from her crown—that appeared around the corner.

"Hey, girl!" she cried, and waved me in. She was sitting on the floor. At least three people and one dog were sprawled in a pile on the bed. The room was done in classic squat style: crudely sheetrocked walls, no joint tape or paint, drooping plastic over pink insulation on the ceiling, clothes and books scattered on the plywood floor. There was a loud fan in the window, pulling in more hot air.

"I forgot all about these!" Raven said when I handed her the books.

I eased down next to her on the floor, stiff and awkward. My body didn't fold up all supple like Raven's. She had her legs stretched out in front of her like a dancer and I remembered her telling some square girls carrying mats on St. Mark's that it was fucked up for Westerners to do yoga, it was like culture stealing.

"These shitheads took all the QFT that was left." Raven gestured at the bed, clicking her tongue piercing against the rings in her lip.

"Q what?"

"Horse tranquilizers." Raven looked at the bed longingly. "That was good shit."

"What're you working on?"

She looked down at the pile of jeans on her lap. "Abby gave me this patch." She held it up: *Eat the Rich*. "But I keep sewing the legs together."

"Give it here." I wiped my sweaty hands on my T-shirt, then cut her thread with my Leatherman so I could start over. "Have you heard of this squat called the Bakery in Williamsburg?"

I slipped one of her paperbacks into the jeans to keep the needle from going through the leg.

"You're a fucking genius!" Raven said. "Brooklyn? Yeah, wait . . ." She nudged the bed with a very dirty, very tan bare foot. "That kid Jimmy lives there, right?"

A dark-haired girl murmured without opening her eyes, "Jimmy Hey?"

"No, punker Jimmy with the hair." Raven waved a hand around her forehead. "Didn't he move out there?" To me she added, "He was staying here last year in Gibby's space."

"Oh, right," Lee, a big guy with long dreads, chuckled, "the laaaadies' man."

"I didn't meet Jimmy." I made quick stitches around the patch.

Raven watched over my shoulder. "Jimmy's a total fashion punk, and he's always got girls all over him. Everyone thought he was with Abby and then he brought this chick back here one night, the bartender from Sophie's, you know that, like, biker-looking girl? And Abby kicked up a shit-fit and wouldn't let them in the house, and the whole block was outside and the cops came and everything. It was nuts. Abby got him kicked out."

"Oh, great."

"Why?"

"I guess me and this kid Lorenzo are moving in there. To the Bakery squat."

"Oh rad, you got a *house!*" She leaned back to give me a high five. "Lorenzo from Disguerro?"

"Yeah." I smiled at the patch, liking how that sounded.

"No shit, I saw him earlier."

"You did?"

"He was with that girl from Dos Blocos . . . what's her name, with the little dog? Did she and Brian break up?"

"I wouldn't know." I pulled the thread into a knot and handed her the jeans.

"Kick *ass!*" Raven jumped up and pulled her shorts off. She wasn't wearing underwear. Somehow, being so lithe and sun-browned, she made being naked look innocent and childlike. She shimmied into the jeans and twisted around to look at the new patch, blending in with all the others.

A pretty girl with white-blond hair and tiny dots tattooed up her sides leaned in the doorway. Abby. I'd met her before but she didn't look at me. There were other people with her. "You coming, Raven?"

Raven dropped down to give me a hug. "Sid, thanks, babe, I gotta go!"

I heard her voice float down the stairs, her footsteps mingling with those of people I didn't know. I stuck Raven's sewing needle carefully into her spool of thread and looked for someplace safe to put it.

"Is this a bad time?" I asked Veronica from the pay phone on her corner a couple blocks south of Rot-Squat. No, it was perfect, she just needed half a dozen things from the deli. Of course I could get them for her, what else did I have to do? Her explanation of which deli to go to and which deli not to go to took so long it cost me another quarter. And then I stood in front of 9th Street Squat waiting for what felt like forever, too cheap to waste another quarter. I wasn't going to yell up to the fourth floor either; this building intimidated me too much. I just stood there sweating until Veronica leaned out her window.

"I couldn't get off the phone!" She tossed down the key in a sock with an easy shrug.

I let myself in and climbed the wide stairs. I had been here to a workday earlier in the summer, naive enough to think I could ease into a space that way. It was totally out of my league. Over the years the squatters had rebuilt this whole building—floors, walls, plumbing, electricity—all to code. It looked like a real apartment building inside, every space had a locked door and its own bathroom. The condescending guy who "orientated" all of us for the workday said the building was looking for a family of color with young children for the next open apartment, to improve diversity. But we could put in some hours anyway. It would be noted. It would have been a total waste of time if I hadn't met Veronica. She was all into it that I was a single woman who was tough and wanted to squat. She was so cool, with her huge necklaces and hair wrapped in a big scarf and cordless drill on a holster on her hip. Instead of acting like a guy, she made working with power tools look femme.

I sipped herbal iced tea at her table while Veronica worked in her kitchen. "Brooklyn!" She waved her whisk in the air, "Of course! I *knew* that was the place for you."

"Yeah?"

"I mean, forget the city unless you were here years ago. Seriously. You're going to *love* Brooklyn."

I looked at her skeptically while she poured batter into a pan. Brooklyn wasn't a prize. We both knew that. She was surprised I'd found anything at all.

She slammed the oven door and settled across from me at the table, fanning her face. "It's too hot to be baking, I don't know why I said I'd make a cobbler. It's Jessie's birthday. You know Jessie? No? Anyways, that happened fast, huh? What's their process, are you a full house member?"

"Oh, well . . ." I thought of my long silent walk down two flights of stairs with Mitch and wondered how I'd even dare go back there again.

"Find out. Seriously. It'd suck if you put a lot of work in and then you find out you've been on trial or something."

"I don't think it's like . . . that formal . . ."

"What are they, consensus? Majority?" She leaned forward on her arms, looking at me through her little cat-eye glasses. "Will you have say in adding new house members or are they, like, going to offer a room to any Joe who wanders in?"

I bit my lip. "That's a good question."

She lifted her dreads off the back of her neck, twisting them into a tighter knot on top of her head. Her armpits were unshaven. "The city must own the building, right? Since it's been squatted a few months already? I mean, it's got to be like on the Lower East Side, right, or is it different out there, can you squat privately owned stuff?"

"Oh, I don't—"

When Veronica's timer dinged I felt like a relieved kid at the final bell. She put her cake pan in a basket and we walked down the well-lit stairs together. She was heading east to Avenue D, and assuming I was going to the L train, she asked me to post a letter on 14th Street. I wasn't headed that way but I didn't tell her. It was easier just to do it.

When I got back to ABC No Rio and climbed up to the roof, I was exhausted and it wasn't even dark yet. I flopped down on top of my sleeping bag. Looking south I could see the Williamsburg Bridge, steel and lights, rising up above the buildings. I had to go for it. This was the only chance that had come my way after three months in the city. I had to make it work, no matter how awkward or hard it might be. With Lorenzo or without. What was the alternative? Staying here on the roof, sweating my ass off, waking up at dawn with the sun, waiting for winter to come? I rolled up my sleeping bag and walked to the J train.

On Rodney Street I heard my name. Skip waved from the basketball court next to the highway, still in his dress shoes, with a sweatband around his stringy hair. Mitch dribbled a ball. He was wearing green nylon shorts with his Air Jordans. He jumped to make a shot, his knees together.

"You play horse?" Skip cupped his hands around his mouth so I could hear him over the traffic.

I dropped my backpack by the edge of the chain-link fence and pushed my armbands and bracelets up my wrists. Mitch tossed the ball and it landed in my hands with a satisfying thump. I bounced it a few times to get the feel. Mitch was so tall, of course basketball was his game. I liked volleyball better. In junior high I'd been on my school's team. But since I always hung out with guys, I could shoot hoops and play pool and I wasn't half bad at hacky sack. I lined up the shot, squinting to see the hoop in the dusk. I threw from deep in my shoulder. The ball hit the backboard, bounced on the rim, and dropped through the net. I raised my arms over my head in victory and felt the first cool breeze of the evening drifting over the BQE.

III

"Lorenzo came by earlier," Skip whispered. It was trash night and we were sneaking the bags I'd filled out of the Bakery.

"He did?" I asked, startled to hear the name in my thoughts spoken aloud.

"I told him you were sleeping up on the second floor for now. He put his stuff up there too."

"I guess that means he'll be back sometime." I was totally disappointed. I'd barely left the house in three days. If I hadn't gone out for food earlier, I could have seen him, asked what was going on.

Skip glanced at me. "You guys aren't a couple, are you?"

"No."

"That's good."

"Good?"

Skip heaved his bag on top of a neighbor's broken dresser. He had said that if we added a couple of bags to the piles in front of each building, no one would notice. I shoved mine into the same pile and put a bundle of magazines on top of it and looked up at the building. No movement. We headed back to the house for more.

"Oh yeah, couples are really bad for a group house,"

Skip said. "Everyone is equal and friends until there's a couple. They just agree on everything together."

"And everyone else is left out." I thought of my Dad and Angela, how I'd suddenly become a third wheel when they met.

"Exactly. They just want to spend *all* their time together!"

He sounded perplexed by the thought. I had wondered if he was gay, but now I reconsidered. "You into straight edge?" I asked. I heaved a bag over my shoulder so it rested on my back and we headed up Rodney to Hope Street, where Skip said he'd seen a dumpster.

"Straight what?" He held his own bag awkwardly in front of him so it hit his shins.

"Straight edge? Youth of Today? Minor Threat?"

"I don't . . . What's that?"

"Bands, hardcore, you know . . ."

The dumpster was in front of a building under construction. I swung my bag over the edge and we both flinched when it landed, but no lights came on in the dark block. Skip had trouble heaving his in. I got my hands under it and helped push it over. I had at least fifty pounds on wiry little Skip.

"You never heard of Black Flag?" A squatter who didn't know anything about punk was a surprise to me. "Agnostic Front?"

"Sorry, I'm not hip, I guess. Why did you think I was into that?"

"Oh . . . well . . ." Good question. How had we gotten into this? "What you said about couples, I guess . . . I thought of straight edge. Some straight edge kids are celibate."

"Celibate?"

"You know . . ." I felt awkward; I was glad Rodney Street was so dark. "Mostly they just don't drink or do drugs. The idea is being clean so you can, like, think straight. I just thought when you were down on relationships, maybe . . ."

"Are *you* straight edge?" Skip looked at me as he unlocked the front door.

"No, I don't call myself that. I don't eat meat, but . . . I'm not into Krishna or anything." I shrugged. I *had* been celibate all summer, but it wasn't by choice. I pulled more bags out of the first floor and gave the lighter one to Skip. It was so cool he was helping with this gross sweaty work.

I started to thank him as we headed across South 1st but he interrupted, "Hare Krishna? Like the orange robe guys?"

"That scene is totally weird," I said. I dropped my bag in front of the house directly across the street. We were getting tired, and their pile wasn't too big. "I don't get why punk kids would get into Krishna. I think all organized religion is messed up, you know?"

"Exactly! That's just what I think!" Skip put his bag next to mine and smiled up at the house behind it with his open, defenseless face. "Wow, Sid, it's really great to have an intellectual around."

* * *

I decided the second floor needed a mural. The east wall was an expanse of white plaster, empty and inviting. A mural would make the house feel more like a squat. I sat on my sleeping bag and doodled ideas in my sketchbook. If downstairs was where the bakery ovens had once been, this floor must have been used for packaging, with the walls of windows for natural light. There were two small offices at the back with frosted glass doors. Skip lived in one and Eddie in the other. Eddie's door was open, his radio a drone of baseball. He was lifting weights and every time I looked in his direction, he was grinning at me with his red strained face. I wanted to move my sleeping bag so I was out of his line of sight, but I was worried that would seem rude.

When I had a drawing I liked, I took the lamp over to the plaster wall. I had painted a mural at my high school in Connecticut. The theme was *Alice in Wonderland*. My friends and I thought the adults wouldn't get the drug references. We thought we were smarter than everyone else, listening to the Velvet Underground and passing a joint while we painted giant mushrooms and drink-me bottles. That was before I started going to all-ages punk shows. For my friends at school, the Velvet Underground turned into the Doors, then the Grateful Dead. Pot started looking like a gateway drug to shitty music. The hardcore kids I met at shows didn't care much about drugs either way, they just wanted to save their money for demo tapes and band T-shirts and vegan burritos.

I used a crayon to start sketching on the wall. Eddie came meandering out of his room holding dumbbells to see what I was doing. He hunched on a milk crate doing curls in the dark. Drawing on the white wall with the light on me, it was like I was on stage.

"Who's winning the game?" I asked to make conversation.

"Huh?"

"Never mind." I drew a huge egg shape in the center of the wall and then a horizon line. I was sore from working downstairs all week; stretching my arms over my head felt good. The front door creaked open downstairs and I held my breath, listening to the bolt click back in place. I hoped it was Lorenzo, though it didn't seem likely he had a key yet, and the bouncing steps on the stairs didn't sound like him, he was more of a trudger.

A lanky boy with Manic Panic red hair burst into the room behind a pizza box. I hadn't met him yet, but I knew right away it was Jimmy. The ladies' man, the fashion punk from Ohio, the kind of skate punk with bangs and a Dead Kennedy's shirt who all the cheerleaders wanted to date in high school. He was hardly ever here at the squat, he spent most nights at the apartments of girlfriends and buddies, wherever there was a PlayStation and food to mooch.

Jimmy cocked his head at me and pulled off his headphones. He gestured at Eddie, who had finished working out and was stretched flat on the dirty floor, arms crossed on his stomach, asleep. "You slip him a mickey or what?"

Skip poked his head out of his room at the sound of Jimmy's voice.

"Skippy, my man." Jimmy held up the pizza box. "Check this out! Dudes were closing for the night and gave me all this!" He plopped down on the floor in front of the wall facing me, his long legs spread wide around the pizza box.

Skip padded up in his sports socks, feet turned out like a duck, and introduced me in his formal way. "Sid and her friend Lorenzo are going to be living on the first floor." I was hungry. I left the circle of light that made the plaster wall look like a stage set and crouched by the pizza box. I picked the pepperoni off a slice.

"Whoa, downstairs!" Jimmy raised his eyebrows, "Total shithole, right?"

"I know you," I told Jimmy. "I work Donny's table at ABC." I'd seen him around but I'd never have pegged him as a squatter. He was too clean and his look was more Sex Pistols than Crass.

Jimmy picked up my discarded pepperoni and ate them while he studied me. But he didn't recognize me. When you're fat, you're invisible. "So, where's your buddy then?" he asked.

"Um . . . band practice."

"Ha!" Jimmy snickered. "Leaving the dirty work to you, huh?"

Dirty, you could say that again. We didn't have run-

ning water in the house or a mirror. I'd washed up using my gallon jug of drinking water from the deli, but I
didn't want to waste any. It cost money and I'd just get
filthy again tomorrow.

"This drawing is great!" Skip was studying my sketch
on the wall. "Wow, you really know how to draw."

"What's it supposed to be?" Jimmy asked.

"Giuliani." I pointed to the egg shape. "See, he's
Humpty Dumpty, sitting on the brick wall. Headed for
a fall."

"What, over there?"

"No, in the middle. His men are the cops over here.
They're going to give that punk in the corner a ticket for
drinking beer on the street."

"It's looking like a squat in here!" Jimmy laughed.
He had finished his slice and now he aimed his crust at
Humpty Dumpty's face. "Take that, Rudy!"

"Jimmy," Skip said, licking his fingers, "Sid was telling me about how the squats in the city have workdays
where everyone works together on house projects."

Jimmy ripped a piece of crust off another slice and,
squinting one eye, aimed for the cops. "Fuck the *po*-lice!"
he chanted like Ice-T.

"Maybe Sunday?" Skip suggested. "What do you
think?"

Jimmy looked between him and me like he was trying to think of something funny to say. "What did Mitch
say?"

Skip stared at the wall in silence. For some reason

the mention of Mitch ended the conversation. I went back to sketching on the wall. Jimmy finished another slice and threw his crust half-heartedly at the cops. It landed on the floor.

Downstairs the door slammed again and we listened to feet coming up the stairs. Mitch, in his basketball sneakers and jeans, rounded the corner and the light caught him dramatically. He and I were spotlit on stage together and no one else spoke, so I waved my crayon and said, "Hiya!"

Mitch's eyes scanned the wall as he crossed the floor. I felt suddenly silly, like decorating the house, when there was so much real work to do, was frivolous. Mitch's sneaker hit Jimmy's pizza crust and he paused a moment to look down.

"You're gonna get rats in here," he said. Then he disappeared up the next flight of stairs.

Eddie sighed in his sleep, still stretched out on the floor with his ankles crossed, and we all turned to look at him.

Jimmy unfurled, stretching his arms up to the ceiling. "Hittin' the hay, comrades!"

Skip said goodnight too, carefully shutting his door. I picked up the box and collected the leftover crusts in it. I took it downstairs before I went to bed.

In the morning it looked like a moose had ravaged the pizza box. The crusts were gone and the wax paper was shredded into a soft ball of fluff. I shoved the whole mess into a garbage bag and wiped my hands on my shorts. I should have been more grossed out, but I was getting used to it down here.

Mitch appeared in the doorway in a Patriots T-shirt, the messenger bag he took to work slung over his shoulder.

I had all the junk sorted enough that you could walk through the space now, and he followed the path I'd made toward the back wall.

"I'm putting in a woodstove upstairs," he said, "so save me any wood scraps you got." He navigated through the room to a closet and moved a rotten piece of plywood. "Bingo! I knew there was a toilet down here!"

I'd built a sort of barricade around the old toilet with tall wood and pieces of metal. We didn't have running water and it was crusty and gross. Mitch put his bag on the floor and started moving everything.

"You can bucket flush," he said. "Clean it up and find a bucket. I'll show you how to get water at the hydrant. You're gonna be in business."

I stood back, sure I'd get in his way if I tried to help. "Hey, so Skip and I were talking last night. We want to get a house workday going, you know, maybe work on some projects in communal spaces in the building . . ."

Mitch snorted. He lifted a rusty piece of iron, his arms straining. "I live here 'cause I like to be independent, this isn't some hippie *commune*." He wiped his hands on his jeans. "Everybody should know enough to take care of what needs to get done. If they don't, they don't belong here."

"I just thought it'd be, like . . . cool . . . I mean, being new here . . ."

"So we should sit in a circle and hold hands? Tell our life stories?" He strode out the door swinging his bag over his shoulder. It was easy to end up talking to Mitch's back. Like I even wanted to hear his stupid life story.

The door to the laundromat opened and Lorenzo ducked in out of the rain. I dropped the tattered *People* I was flipping through. Even in the fluorescent-lit tan and orange laundromat the guy managed to look cool. He was wearing a filthy Amebix T-shirt and army pants and leather bands on his wrist. If my T-shirt got that dirty the Latino girls on the street scowled and veered their baby carriages away from me, but on him it looked tough.

"Hey, stranger," I said as nonchalantly as I could. My heart pounded. "Skip tell you I was here?"

"Yeah." He sat down a few seats away. "Dude's all agitated."

"There was a workday yesterday. At the house."

"Crap," Lorenzo said. "Everyone was there?"

"No." The workday thing was my idea so I was duty-bound to be there and to drink with Skip at the end of the day, since he'd gotten beer and ice to make it festive. I was paying for my forced cheerfulness now, hung over and irritable. "I told Skip you had to work."

Lorenzo smiled. "Where was everyone else?"

"Mitch thinks he's too good for group projects. So

Jimmy didn't bother showing his face either. He's *never* around, I might add. Really, Mitch is kind of a bully. Skip says—"

"Whoa, *tranquilo*." Lorenzo put out a hand to slow me down. "You gotta stay out of that shit."

Right. Mr. Also-Never-Around. "Seriously," I insisted, "Mitch is so high and mighty, what's the point of living in a squat and being all superior like that?"

Lorenzo frowned. "I don't think he's someone you want to piss off."

I got up and looked into my dryer where the blankets I'd found on the street rose and fell. Lorenzo was right, though in reality none of this was what was really upsetting me.

"You wanted a house, right?" Lorenzo said. I could see his reflection in the dryer, his arms stretched casually along the plastic seat backs. "Now what you want?"

My dryer stopped and I stared into it feeling close to tears. What I wanted was for him to be here with me, doing this together, but I couldn't say that. What right did I have? I was scared I'd only push him away.

"Here, give me." Lorenzo bundled the blankets together and led the way outside. The rain had slowed to a drizzle. We crossed the street dodging puddles.

"I thought I'd hang the blankets in the doorway," I said. "Keep the chill out when it gets cold?"

"Good idea." Lorenzo studied the faded letters painted on the brick while I unlocked the bolt. *Sunshine Crust Baking Factory est. 1944.*

"The Crust Factory," he said. "Where's the crust punks at?"

"I guess that'd be us," I said and sighed.

"Gotta represent." He gave me that smile that made everything better.

Inside, I saw he had left a new toolbox by the door.

"Will you look at the window? I can't get it open." We went through the maze of crap all the way to the back. The window faced a courtyard next door where a retired cop lived. He was cool, Skip said. He'd told Skip and Eddie about when our house used to be a bakery. He said truck drivers would pull off the BQE at dawn for fresh donuts.

"Was just you and Skip at the workday?" Lorenzo asked.

"And Eddie. But he just stood around like he didn't want to get his pants dirty. He told us stories about this junkie squat he lived at in Harlem."

"Yeah?" Lorenzo had WD-40 in his toolbox and big pliers.

"They couldn't afford nails so they built walls by cutting wood too long so it would just hold wedged together with the tension."

Lorenzo laughed. "Oh man. We live with the Loony Toons, huh? It okay staying upstairs?"

"It'll be better when we can move down here."

"Look, I been busy with my band." Lorenzo glanced over his shoulder at me. "We got a show in a coupla weeks."

Here it comes, I thought. He's bailing. I chewed my lip. Why had I said *we* like that, like I was depending on him? Why was I complaining about the guys here and making it sound bad?

"After that," he went on, "I be around more. But man, you kickin' ass down here."

"Really?" I breathed out.

"You done a lot. It's cool."

It was all worth it. We were going to be together here. Lorenzo grunted with effort and the window opened. There was nothing to look at, it faced a brick building, but a gust of air came into the dank room and we leaned into it.

IV

Skip asked if I wanted to go to a poetry slam with him and I dropped the broom I was pushing around and ran to get ready. I had to laugh at myself while I dug in my bag for a clean shirt. I always said poetry was for beatnik throwbacks, but I really needed to get out of the house. Over the last few weeks I'd gotten the first floor livable and moved in, but it wasn't the fun, friend-filled world I'd dreamed squatting would be. Lorenzo was home one night out of three, Jimmy even less. I avoided Mitch because he was so judgmental and Eddie because he was vacant and weird. I wanted Veronica and Raven to come visit but they both acted like Brooklyn was on the other side of the moon.

On the L train into the city, Skip seemed nervous. He was muttering to himself, distracted. We transferred to the 6 at Union Square and got off in the 30s. I followed Skip up Third Ave. and into some place that looked like an Irish sports bar. It was air-conditioned and full of men with crew cuts. I wondered if we were in the wrong place until a skinny guy with a pencil stuck in his hat came rushing from the back.

"Skip! Tell me you're ready." He slapped his clipboard. "I only got the Prozac girl and the angry banker tonight, I'm freakin' out."

"I'm gonna do it," Skip breathed.

The guy clapped Skip's shoulder and snapped his fingers over our heads at the bartender. "Drinks for these two," he cried, spraying me with spit. The bartender served us without carding me.

In a little room in back where chairs circled a microphone, people seemed to know Skip. They held up their drinks or nodded but Skip didn't introduce me to anyone. We found seats and I looked around. Adults with jobs in summer clothes. The kind of squares I wouldn't normally notice. Skip seemed too nervous to talk to me. He sucked on his Corona and studied a piece of wrinkled paper from his pocket.

By the time it was Skip's turn to read, his anxiety had rubbed off on me and I was stiff with embarrassment. He recited with his eyes squeezed shut, intense and weird. At least he didn't rush. Actually, his voice was clear and confident and he knew how to pause for laughs. Laughs! I'd thought he had no sense of humor at all. I looked around and saw that everyone was listening and smiling. His poem was about selling books on the street. That's what he did for work. The refrain was, "I've got books," and at first it was funny, with all the characters passing by who don't care or don't speak English or are in a hurry. The narrator loves his books and calls out his refrain with defiance, but the day is cold, he gets hungry, lonely, bored, yelled at, and by the end,

"I've got books" came out tragic—that's all the guy's got and it's not enough. Skip's shoulders dropped in relief when it was over and everyone hooted. He nodded around the room with stiff jerks of his neck and he gave me a shy smile.

A couple nights later it was Lorenzo's turn to be on stage. Everyone I knew in New York was at his band's first show, even though it was just an early spot at the Spiral. People were curious. Lorenzo's old band from Mexico was notorious and the new singer had been in Five Knive, legendary New York punks. While Lorenzo had been practicing for this show, I had gotten our space together by myself, but watching him play I felt elated. I'd had a tiny role in making this come together and I was proud of it. It was raw, old-school, three-chord punk. They only had twelve songs so it was over in twenty ferocious minutes. Then everyone stood around with their ears ringing saying, "Holy shit!"

"They were *awesome*."

Raven's friends from Rot-Squat gathered in a pack of dreads and jewelry. Abby's skimpy cut-off overalls displayed the row of tiny dots tattooed up her slender sides. A wild mess of white-blond hair hid her face. A girl with dark dreads pulled into a knot wore sports socks with pink pom-poms with her beat-up Adidas and miniskirt. I loved that, it was totally *Mad Max* tennis player. A girl named Jessica wore a dog collar with spikes around her neck.

Once the girls had joined me, Jimmy lost no time sauntering over. He pointed at me with disco fingers, singing, "Housemaaate! Where're y'all going now?" I remembered that he'd had a thing with Abby that had ended badly, but it looked to me like he couldn't take his eyes off her.

I waved over Jimmy's shoulder to Veronica, who stalked toward us in clunky heels and striped knee socks. She gave me a hug, "Not bad for a first show!"

"How's the new job?" I asked her.

Veronica was working construction. Getting jobs wasn't the hard part, plenty of guys thought it was great to get a chick on their crew.

"I thought I'd learn about carpentry but I've just spent, like, two weeks sanding the stair rails," she complained. "Seriously! I'm still on the third floor! The money these jerks spend on their balusters would build a whole house for regular people . . . How's your place coming along?"

"Great! When are you coming to see it?" Out of the corner of my eye I saw Lorenzo leave the stage, sweat and excitement glowing on him, his dreads pushed behind his ears. Kids high-fived as he passed, threading toward me, like he felt the same magnetic pull I did. He winked at me and joy spiked into my brain.

Veronica dangled a key in front of my eyes to get my attention back. "I have my boss's van! We can go now!"

"To Brooklyn?" I clapped my hands. "Jimmy! Lorenzo! Veronica's driving us to Brooklyn!"

Raven cried, "Let's all go!"

Lorenzo led the way out of the club like the Pied Piper. Stumps was out on Houston Street leaning against Veronica's van. He was the guy I thought of as the door-man at Rot-Squat; always on the stoop keeping an eye on things. His housemates told him we were going to Brooklyn and he took charge, directing us all to buy beer at the deli next door because there might not be stores out in Brooklyn. I didn't drink much, one beer would make me giddy, but everyone else grabbed armloads of forties like they were going to be trapped in the bor-oughs for a week.

I sat up front next to Veronica to give directions. Lorenzo leaned between us to talk about the show. I'd never seen him so hyped up. The guitarist had started the second song on the wrong chord, he said. Did we see that kid in front throwing beer around? Did we see the dude from Missing Foundation was there? Lorenzo's euphoria was contagious. This was it, I thought, I'm really doing it. Living in the city, rattling home over the brightly-lit bridge with my friends.

When we pulled up in front of the Bakery, Veronica glanced into the back of the van and saw Stumps swig-ging from a bottle. "Did you guys open beers in the car? I could lose my license!"

Stumps laughed, spewing beer through his gold teeth.

"Sorry," Raven apologized, but Veronica was out al-ready, slamming her door.

Jimmy sang to Stumps, "Bitch alert!" and cackled, *Beavis and Butthead* style.

Inside, I ran to put on some lights while Veronica stood in the doorway. She squinted through her cat-eye glasses at the old braided rug next to my patchwork quilt–covered bed, the lamp on a stack of suitcases. I had made a little island of street-scored hominess adrift in the space. You didn't want to get too near to the crumbling, damp walls. We still had to figure out how to seal them. Lorenzo and I had a line dividing our spaces. It was like *The Brady Bunch*, that episode where they put the masking tape down the middle of the room. But we didn't have tape; just bags of garbage and metal scraps. Way in back, under the window, was Lorenzo's bare mattress and sleeping bag, backpack of clothes, a folding chair.

Lorenzo squeezed past Veronica, followed by everyone else, and turned on his boom box.

Veronica asked to see the rest of the house. "Why don't you have a phone here?" she asked.

"Mitch said he tried and they wanted some big deposit or something . . ."

"Who'd he call? They can't refuse service just because it's a squat."

The stairs were dark and narrow, but when we emerged on the open second floor with streetlights filtering through the windows, we found Skip waiting for us. He looked worried. "What's going on?" he asked.

"Nothing, we just brought some people over." I ran

my hand through my hair. "Lorenzo's band played, so—"

"I didn't know that. Was Jimmy there?"

Crap. Lorenzo had specifically told me not to tell Skip about the show. Lorenzo was all chummy and cool to Skip's face, so Skip thought they were pals.

Veronica saved me by introducing herself. She told Skip she lived at 9th Street Squat, opening with her credentials, and watched his face to gauge his reaction. "When we moved in there, it looked a *lot* worse than this."

"Did you see Sid's mural?" Skip asked, and led her to the wall.

I'd been too busy cleaning out the first floor to work on it since the night I'd started it. You couldn't even see what it was supposed to be, it was just a sketch, but Skip was always talking about it like it proved something about the building. He told Veronica about his vision for the second floor, how it should be an art space, where everyone in the house could work on art projects and collaborate. He used the word *art* like it was religion, which made me cringe. A serious squatter like Veronica would be more impressed if we were running a soup kitchen or teaching bike repair to disadvantaged youth. Finally, I got so uncomfortable I cut Skip off.

"Let's show Veronica upstairs," I suggested.

The third floor was the best part of the house. Jimmy's room was in front, right above the street, and Mitch's room was way in back against the far wall. Between their rooms was a loft-like space with big windows overlooking the BQE. Mitch had installed his woodstove back by the kitchen near his room. At the kitchen table, Mitch, shirtless, was drinking from an orange juice box.

"This would make a better art space than downstairs!" Veronica said. "All those windows! The high ceiling!"

"But the artists should work in the *center* of the house," Skip insisted.

"What's this, an inspection?" Mitch asked.

Skip laughed nervously. "Veronica's from 19th Street Squat."

"It's actually 9th—" I started.

"Whatever." Mitch turned to head into his room. "Maybe she should go back there and tell *them* how to run their building." His pale, naked back was an accusation.

Downstairs, Skip kept apologizing to Veronica for Mitch, making it worse by not letting it go. Veronica crossed her arms and looked bored. In my discomfort, I took the bong Stumps handed me and dragged a long toke. Pot was supposed to relax you, right? Then I passed it to Skip, who, like me, rarely smoked. But I guess he was trying to be cool too. He breathed in and collapsed in a coughing fit.

No one noticed. Jimmy lounged with Lorenzo on Lorenzo's mattress, their eyes heavy and stoned. Raven's girlfriends were dancing to a techno tape, bumping each other and giggling. Stumps mocked them, holding his beer over his head. In the time Veronica and I had been upstairs, everyone had managed to get shit-faced.

"Come on, Lorenzo!" Abby reached down to his bed for him, her voice slurred, ignoring Jimmy.

Raven sat cross-legged on my braided rug, rifling through my box of zines. "You have *Squat Beautiful!*" She waved it at me. "I took pictures in this one, did you see?"

She opened it to portraits of girl train hoppers. I touched the paper and saw from the way it shimmered that I was totally stoned. "These are amazing! I forgot you were a photographer!"

I tried to focus on what Raven was telling me about going to art school and how she'd quit and the photographers she liked, and she seemed utterly beautiful and smart and I loved how her long beaded dreads bobbed around and how her tongue piercing clicked against her lip ring. But I couldn't follow; I was distracted by something bad in my peripheral vision. Skip was telling Veronica about selling books on the street, his voice stumbling all over itself. It must be my ears. I shook my head to make it stop, but I still couldn't concentrate. I worried he was going to recite his poem. The mattress groaned and I jumped.

It was Veronica, moving away from Skip and sinking down next to me, her legs crossed at the knee like an adult in her heeled shoes. She pointed at Lorenzo's mattress where the boys were sprawled. "You and Lorenzo share the room?"

"Well, it's a big space . . ." I glanced at Skip, but he

was rubbing his eyes and didn't seem to be listening.

She raised an eyebrow. "You need a wall."

"I guess . . ." I looked up at the ceiling. I had no idea how to build a wall. I'd talked to Lorenzo about the idea, but he dismissed it. I was secretly pleased that he didn't think it was urgent to separate our spaces.

Abby had Lorenzo on his feet now. He did a comic mosh in a circle around the girls, stomping with his head down. They cheered him on.

Veronica raised her voice over the music: "Seriously, you need a wall."

Raven jumped in: "I've shared spaces with guys before!"

I didn't know everyone was listening but Abby yelled, "You were screwing them all, you *slut!*" and Jimmy whooped from the bed, like he approved of the turn the conversation was taking.

"We don't know what Sid and Lo-*ren*-zo get up to in here," the dog-collar girl sang. She stumbled and grabbed onto Stump's bullet belt for support.

Stumps bumped her hips. "Give you three guesses!"

"Cowabunga!" Jimmy held up his beer like a frat boy.

"*Siiiiid,*" Abby sang. She reached down to me on my bed, her necklaces dancing into my face. "Come on, girl!" I shook my head and tried to smile in a relaxed way. I moshed sometimes at shows, but even watching this sexy-girl techno-thing made me feel like a hippopotamus.

Jimmy made a megaphone with his hands and hooted, "Sid! Sid! Sid!"

Lorenzo had been moshing around like he wasn't hearing any of this, but now he kicked Jimmy's boot where it was hanging off the bed.

"Oh *shiiit*," Abby grinned, like things were getting fun. "Fight!"

"They's fightin' over *yoooou*." Stumps pointed at me, his narrow eyes just slits in his round face.

"You trippin'," Lorenzo growled, and threw his beer bottle at the wall where it shattered near Jimmy's head. The violence of it made everyone jump.

"Jeez, dude! Sorry!" Jimmy held his hands up in playful surrender.

Lorenzo kicked glass out of the way and threw himself down on his mattress, his face angry and dark.

Raven leaned her cheek against my leg and rubbed my knee like she wanted to console me, which only made Lorenzo's anger seem more humiliating.

Veronica stood up. "I gotta go," she said. "These guys can take the train back or whatever."

Skip jumped up. "I'll get the door for you."

In a moment he was back, leaning down to me, his face rippled with tension. "Sid," he hissed, "the *door* was *open*!"

The pot had made him paranoid; his eyes were really red.

"Did you shut it?"

"Yes! But why was it *open*?" He looked around hysterically for intruders. "It's really late! This music is too loud!" He scurried to the boom box.

Raven and I went outside and found the dark-haired Rot-Squat girl around the corner slouched against the building. Her head was buried in her bare knees and her optimistic pink pom-poms looked gray in the dark.

"What happened?" I asked. "Are you sick?"

She nodded and groaned.

Skip came dashing outside and grabbed my arm. "We've got to go inside! The *neighbors!*"

I looked around, exasperated. Our house was the last on the block and over here around the corner, we were just facing the park and the highway. "No one can see us here!"

Skip put his hands in his hair. "Sid, I need your help!"

"Everything's fine! Give us a sec, will you?"

"Fine? Fine?"

"You're freaking out!"

"Oh!" he cried. "Oh! *I'm* the problem?"

A retching sound made us look down.

"Can you get Stumps?" Raven asked me.

I hurried inside, happy to get away from Skip. Now Abby was sitting on Jimmy's lap on Lorenzo's bed, their faces hidden by the cloud of her hair. The dog-collar girl was sprawled on my bed with her sneakers on my pillow. Stumps sat on the floor near her.

"Um, Stumps?" I gestured at the door.

He looked around hazily, noting the absence of his girlfriend, then staggered up, sloshing beer on my bed. "On it, captain!" He saluted and stumbled out.

Skip ran in and pulled the boom box cord out of the

wall. Lorenzo just watched him. The party was over. Lorenzo kicked his mattress and Jimmy and Abby jumped and giggled. "Go upstairs," Lorenzo growled at them.

When they were gone, Lorenzo laid down on his sleeping bag and shut his eyes. The girl on my bed rolled onto her side and snored. I dropped into my velvet armchair and propped my feet up on a corner of the bed.

If only I could sleep. I'd forgotten what pot did to my brain. I had a slide show of every stupid thing I'd ever done in my life. Starting with the first day of third grade at a new school when I thought I'd make a splash by wearing the ten gallon Stetson my dad got me in Texas. God. My face burned again remembering it. Everyone called me Dallas Cowgirl all year.

I was lucky to have a house. I was lucky to live with Lorenzo even if he'd been badgered into being mean tonight. This was my fault, thinking it would be fun to have my friends come see the place. God. I was seriously on crack.

V

"Dude, sounds awesome. Catch you later." From our room I could hear Lorenzo out in the foyer talking to Skip, all buddy-buddy. I was trying to decide which T-shirt to pull over my thermal. Rorschach? Ugh. Laundry pile. At the bottom of my trunk were shirts from bands I didn't even remember seeing.

Some college kid from Tennessee got all excited that I was sitting at Donny's distro table reading *Anna Karenina*. It had been a slow day. He wanted to talk about the political themes and I just wanted to get back to the story. Well, I would be wearing his shirt tonight. I hoped his band didn't suck.

Lorenzo swept back the curtain in the doorway. "Ready?"

We walked up Rodney to where the streets of North and East Williamsburg came together at an angle, colliding like continental plates to form the mountain range of the elevated BQE. Under the highway people skateboarded and slept in boxes. We cut across to North 6th and headed for the river.

Lorenzo walked fast and I matched his pace. "You meeting Skip later?"

He gave me a surprised look, a chewed dreadlock in his mouth. "Fuck no!"

"I thought I heard you making plans."

He scoffed, "Whatever. Just say yes to keep him happy."

"We could have brought him to Donny's," I said, all mock-innocent.

"Everyone thinks Brooklyn squats are bad already!" he exploded, but was also grinning. "We can't let them see Skip! Guy's all weird."

I loved feeling chosen by Lorenzo, it made the night air sweet in my lungs. We hit Bedford and made a right, walking in synch, like when we'd been out looking for buildings. We barely spent time together anymore. He only showed up at the Bakery when he was exhausted and burnt out on people and wanted to sleep and be left alone. I was alone a lot, so I was probably too eager and chatty when he was around. I tried to give him space, but it was disappointing how little energy he had for working on our house and discussing our housemates and exploring Brooklyn. Well, tonight we were together and I felt tall and smart and cool just walking next to him, included in his aura of being always at the center of things.

The landscape opened out into a park. Gigantic trees lined the street, like we were in Paris. There were people walking dogs, a big school with wide steps, and tennis courts.

"You know, it's not really Skip's fault. He had super weird parents."

"You think?" Lorenzo gave me a look.

"They were seriously checked out. He told me one time his mom left him with these people who owned the dry cleaner in town and just disappeared. Some Ukrainian family."

"Whassat?"

"Like, Russians. She barely knew these people and they didn't know what to do or when she was coming back and he wouldn't eat anything 'cause he was scared, and when his mom came back the man yelled at her. It was, like, three days."

The park ended and we were in Greenpoint. Stores had Polish signs and there were big chains that I thought only existed in Manhattan. CVS, Dunkin' Donuts. There were people everywhere: perfumed girls, guys with mustaches, grandmothers in housedresses and pantyhose.

"You think Donny's got the last Dark Throne?" Lorenzo asked.

"What's that, Viking shit? Aren't they all Nazis?"

"It's like crust. Sounds like Final Conflict, you gotta hear it."

Someone we didn't know let us into Donny's loft. In the center of a crowd in the kitchen we found Donny wearing a paper crown and holding a beer. He had played in punk bands in the '80s and lived in a squat on 13th Street.

Donny wrapped me in a bear hug. "The squatters are here!" he cheered. He liked us; we reminded him of the old days.

"There're still squats?" one of his friends asked. "I thought that was over!"

Everyone wanted to know what our neighbors thought of our squat in Brooklyn and I told them about the retired cop next door, who loved that kids were fixing up the empty place. "He let the guys run extension cords to his place for tools," I told them, "before we got our own electric hooked up." We sounded so organized when I explained it like that, with Lorenzo near me, nodding along.

I'd been in Donny's room listening to records and I lost track of time. In the bathroom where beer and ice had been piled in the claw-foot tub there was only a puddle left. The bathroom was huge; there was a worktable and a washing machine. A metal shelf lined with ink and chemicals and plants. A row of silkscreen frames Donny used to print shirts for bands. In the mirror I saw my face was flushed and relaxed from the unaccustomed warmth. I wandered back into the kitchen. Empty bottles covered the counter. I drank a glass of water leaning over the sink. What a luxury, running water. Glasses.

I found Lorenzo up on the roof in a cloud of pot smoke with two leggy girls. I'd met them earlier, they lived in a loft close by. They were huddled against the low wall at the edge of the flat roof. When the door slammed behind me they turned together in slow motion.

"You ready to head out?" I asked Lorenzo, rubbing my arms in the chilly night. I ignored the eyes of the girl in the red clown shoes and striped tights. Up and down she scanned me.

Lorenzo cleared his throat but couldn't get a word out. The blond girl in the fur hat poked him and snickered. "Dude," he finally managed, "nah, you go . . . ahead."

"I don't know how to get back!"

"It's easy, you go . . . like . . ." He pointed away from the city skyline behind him, not looking at me. "That way . . ."

The girls buried their faces in his shoulders, helpless with laughter. Fine. I'd leave him. See how he liked that.

When Lorenzo turned up a couple days later, he was with a band from Spain that needed somewhere to crash. I didn't mention getting lost on the way back from Greenpoint, that it took me two hours to get home, that I'd ended up on Bushwick Avenue. What was there to say?

The band kicked rubble out of the way and spread sleeping bags around Lorenzo's side of the room and we all stayed up late drinking beer and listening to tapes. They spoke Spanish and I tried to follow. They screamed with laughter at something and I nudged the green-haired singer to translate.

"Fucking Emilio," he sputtered, "he no take his boots off never!"

"Since when?" I asked.

"Since we get in America! Three weeks!"

They hooted. One of his comrades leaned over him,

trying to grab at a boot and Emilio kicked him hard. The guy stumbled over a chunk of metal and crashed into the wall. They all laughed louder. The guy lay there cursing until someone handed him a beer. I went to bed around three. Someone turned the tape up and I wrapped a pillow around my head.

I didn't want to make noise when I got up the next afternoon, they'd probably sleep all day. So I left the Bakery and went out. It was true what Veronica had said: now that we were both around, we really needed our own rooms. There was just so much I couldn't do on my own, but I couldn't bug Lorenzo about helping me build a wall anymore. He'd started getting irritable when I asked for help, like he thought I was a nag.

I walked through East Williamsburg on Devoe Street. It was mostly Italian and there were old-world Christmas decorations everywhere. Garlands over the street, colored lights. It would be fun to get a tree for our house; maybe we could steal one late at night. My dad and I never got a tree when I was a kid. We always lived in temporary apartments, sometimes construction trailers on job sites. He managed a crew that installed cable and we lived like nomads; ten months in one town, six in the next. When I was in high school we ended up in Connecticut. I wonder if I would have gotten into hardcore and punk if not for the Anthrax club being down the street. I learned about everything there. Then Dad met Angela. My last year of high school, he was in Baltimore with her so much I basically lived alone and cut school to go to New York and see shows at CBs or ABC whenever I wanted.

I'd just gotten a letter from my dad, inviting me to Angela's place for Christmas. I didn't think I'd go. It was lame how my dad had moved in with her the instant I moved to New York, like they were just waiting for me to get lost. At least the letter was helpful. Mostly I used Donny's PO box on 14th Street, but I'd asked my dad to write to the Bakery because the library wanted something postmarked for proof of address. I got a library card and spent the afternoon reading about home repair and construction.

On my way home I ran into one of the Spanish dudes. I spotted him from a block away on Grand Avenue, a ratty punk with tight jeans and boots and a million rings through his face. My heart lifted at the sight of a comrade out here in Brooklyn. I took him to the Key Foods where the beer was cheapest and we walked back to the Bakery in the dusk. He was the drummer. He was trying to tell me what an asshole their singer was. Or maybe he meant their old singer. It was hard to follow, and I don't think it was just a language problem.

The next day Mitch took me aside. "If you need me to say something to Lorenzo, I will."

"About what?" I was totally caught off guard. Mitch barely spoke to anyone in the house; we were lucky to get a nod out of him. What could he possibly say to Lorenzo that I couldn't?

Mitch's deep-set, bruised-looking eyes narrowed. "Those dudes. It's pretty loud and crazy down there. I don't want to see Lorenzo take advantage of you."

Unbelievable. "Take *advantage* of me? Because a girl doesn't like to party, right? She has to be protected, right?"

"I didn't say that."

"Would you ask me that if I wasn't a girl?"

Mitch crossed his arms. "Well, maybe if you weren't a girl you wouldn't put up with his bullshit! Do you even speak Spanish?"

I crossed my arms like he had, and assumed a skeptical look, but the question chilled me.

Mitch clenched his jaw and threw an angry look in the direction of Eddie's room. "We *heard* them," he said in a low voice. "Everyone heard them. We don't like how they're talking about . . ." He stalled, embarrassed.

About *me*, he must mean, but he couldn't bring himself to say it. Eddie, Skip . . . Oh god, the whole house was discussing this? I was mortified but I stared into Mitch's face. I wouldn't show it. "What did they say?"

Mitch looked at the floor. I watched his pale face turn red and a pit opened up in my belly. "There were some, some personal comments," he stammered, "about . . . uh . . ."

"Why don't you mind your own business?" My voice came out strange and high and I turned on my heel and ran.

* * *

I woke up on Sunday and looked at my watch. Noon. By the time everyone was up, it would be too dark and cold to get anything done. Why was I being polite to them, when they were talking shit about me so my whole house could hear? The bathroom was disgusting, there were empty cans and bottles everywhere, the few dishes we had were buried under pizza boxes and sandwich wrappers. It was time to clean.

I needed water and I had to step over a snorting, smelly Spaniard, the one with the boots, to get to a water bucket. He didn't stir. There were beer cans in the bucket, like someone had made an attempt to collect garbage. Amazing. I set them quietly against the wall, in the sea of other empties.

In the foyer by the front door I found the metal bar that opened the hydrant. We were supposed to hang it on a nail by the door but it was usually on the floor somewhere. I walked up Rodney Street swinging my bucket, the metal bar over my shoulder. Traffic on the BQE was light. The sun was bright for December, it wasn't cold, really, just brisk. The hydrant was on a weedy triangular spit between a BQE off-ramp and Rodney. Mitch had explained that the way the fire department opened hydrants was with a huge magnet. There was a hidden cylinder inside the main cylinder and the magnet made them lock together and turn at the same time. Mitch had drilled a hole in the hydrant and slipped in a long nail. Then this special long wrench could be used to turn the two cylinders together. It was easy, unless the last person to get water had been Mitch. He cranked it shut so tight I had to throw all my weight into it. It finally budged with a satisfying creak. I filled my bucket and felt the sunshine soak into the back of my hoodie. A kid in a U-Haul pulling off the highway waved at me. I held up my hand and my silver skull rings caught the sunlight. I cranked the hydrant shut as tight as I could. I imagined that Mitch would be the next person getting water, and he'd be impressed at how hard it was to open.

I struggled with the heavy bucket into the house, soaking my boots. I hung the bar on its nail but it slipped and fell, hitting a pipe with a loud clang.

I lugged the bucket to the toilet. Lorenzo and his friends never flushed, it was foul. Why couldn't they go get water, what else did they have to do?

"Whas'a fucking racket?" Lorenzo growled from his sleeping bag.

"Sorry," I called on reflex, and then I was even more annoyed. Why was I apologizing? "Just cleaning up after everyone!"

Lorenzo sat up in bed and reached for his boots. "Fucking chill out, Sid," he hissed. He'd started saying that so much, it was like a tic.

"Chill out? Me chill out? Excuse me for living, but I worked my ass off to make this space livable and—"

"You wanna work your ass off," his lip curled meanly, "you gotta lotta work to do." It slipped out of him so easily. It had to be the kind of talk that had been whizzing over my head in Spanish for days.

"What did you say to me?" I stood on the line between our rooms.

He came toward me, as angry as I was, his neck taut.
"You a fuckin' drag, bitchin' all the time."

"I'm a drag? Me? Trying to keep our house from being a shithole?"

"Yeah!" Lorenzo yelled. His friends stirred. The
green-haired guy opened his eyes. Lorenzo stepped
closer and threw an arm at the door like he was shooing
me away. "Get the fuck outta here! Leave me alone!"

"This is my house!"

"Well, get a fuckin' life! All you do's hang around!"
Lorenzo's face was red and twisted close to me.

"Oh, I should start some cool band, right, like you?
Drink beer all night with my jerk-face friends?"

"Do *somethin'*, you loser!"

My arm shot out from my side like someone else
controlled it. My fist, spiked with rings, slammed into
the side of Lorenzo's head and he staggered. I felt the
impact all the way to my shoulder and tingling down
my side. Lorenzo's mouth fell open in shock. He moved
his hand slowly from his temple, and I saw blood. I ran
from the room, terrified.

I almost collided with Mitch on the second floor,
he was on his way down, sneakers unlaced over sweat-
pants. "That yelling . . . Are you okay?"

"Lorenzo . . ." my voice broke into a sob. "He . . ."

Mitch's lips set in a harsh line and he pushed past
me down the stairs. I ran blindly up. Everyone hung out

on the third floor by Mitch's woodstove when it was cold.

Eddie was there now holding out a chair for me. "Lovers' quarrel?"

That made me cry harder. I put my head in my hands. The hatred I had seen in Lorenzo . . . It didn't make any sense; it couldn't be real.

Eddie patted my shoulder. He lit a cigarette and watched the fire while I tried to get control of myself. I wiped my nose on the sleeve of my hoodie.

Mitch came trooping back up the stairs slowly. He didn't look at me. He crouched to put wood on the fire.

"What? What did he say?"

"Well," Mitch kept his back to me, "it sounds like you can take care of yourself."

"What?" I sat up straight. I don't know what I had expected from Mitch, but I felt desperate. "Mitch, what'd he say? What should we . . . ? I can't . . ."

Eddie put out a steadying hand. "Take it easy, now."

Mitch raised himself slowly. "What do you want me to do?"

I almost said, *Kick him out*, but I bit my tongue. If anyone was going to get kicked out, it would be me, I was the one who had gotten violent. It was the kind of thing that could get you instantly thrown out in some squats. If I got any leeway, it would only be because I was a girl. And also, I didn't want Lorenzo gone. I wanted him here and I wanted him to like me again. I started sniffling and Mitch strode back to his room and shut his door.

A little later Eddie went to the corner bodega. "They gone now, yo," he said when he came back with a bagel and milky sweet tea for me, "It's all quiet down there."

He put his feet on a crate of scrap wood and worked a word search puzzle. Mitch's room was silent.

The room got darker and colder and I had no idea what to do. If I went downstairs, Lorenzo and his friends would come home and humiliate me some more. What if he threw me out on the street, while the guys upstairs shrugged and said: *Domestic situation, let them work it out?* I could sleep on the second floor, like when we first moved in, but then wouldn't I be sending a message that Lorenzo was in the right? That I was letting him have our floor? After all the work I'd done! And would Skip even let me stay up there? Would he be on my side? We weren't so friendly lately. Skip might take Lorenzo's side.

I needed a plan, but I was too upset to think straight. So I went downstairs and threw things in a backpack and hurried to the subway station in the dark.

VI

I gave up trying to sleep. The guest room in Angela's condo was so tiny, I could reach the lamp on her desk from the foldout couch. I perused the bookshelves that lined the room by propping myself up on one arm, still under the covers. I'd finished my dad's Hemingway and Steinbeck. Now I was working my way through Angela's Jackie Collins and Danielle Steele. Things were devolving. I'd been in Baltimore since before Christmas, over two weeks.

Four a.m. The clock was sitting next to a depressing pile of books. *Write for Kids*, *Author's Marketplace*. She was going to make a new career for herself with a children's book about a beaver that couldn't build a dam. That is, if I ever left and she got her office back. I'd heard them arguing about it. My dad, placating, offered to move her computer somewhere else while I was there. But there wasn't anywhere else for it in the tiny condo.

I knew I should go back to Brooklyn—there wasn't room for me here. But how could I share a floor with Lorenzo if he hated me, and the whole house knew it? If we couldn't live together, then who got the space and who had to leave? Had I already forfeited it by disappearing and telling no one where I was? By hitting him? I cringed at the memory.

Some nights I could convince myself that by staying away from the Bakery, I was making Lorenzo miss me. He'd be so relieved when I got back, he'd welcome me with open arms. I'd be forgiving but firm, telling him we had to build a wall between our rooms, so we didn't get on each other's nerves again. Then we would live happily ever after. What were the chances it would go like that? I had a recurring dream in which I went back to the Bakery and the locks were changed and no one knew who I was.

I pulled on my hoodie and went to the kitchen with my sketchbook to make hot cocoa. While I stood at the microwave, my dad padded into the kitchen in a robe and slippers, things he'd never owned before he married Angela. If I weren't so depressed I'd tease him for looking like Ward Cleaver.

"Can't sleep, kiddo?" He sat down at the table in front of my sketchbook and peered at the drawing I'd been working on. It was a fantasy version of how my room at the Bakery could be, with a loft bed I wanted to build against a new wall dividing my half of the room from Lorenzo's. "This the much-celebrated domicile?"

"*Was*," I said gloomily.

"Don't tell me you're done squatting already!"

My dad and I were always upbeat with each other. It was like a rule: no complaining. So I didn't know what to say.

"Is this about the Mexican guitar player? Your letters were all full of him and you haven't mentioned him since you got here."

"Bass," I said.

"What?"

"He plays *bass*."

"Isn't a bass a guitar?"

I sat down at the table and blew on my cocoa.

"Think you guys'll patch things up?" he asked.

"No." I thought of Lorenzo taking my hand that night in the Chimney. God. I was so pathetic. I'd stuck around for months hoping for more. But that was it.

"So you're giving up on the house too? That's it?" He paused. "Well, what about this utopia you were so excited about?" He wasn't making fun of me. He looked worried. He liked how idealistic and independent I was and how I got excited about stuff. He'd let me go see bands whenever I wanted, he'd helped me staple my zines.

"Squatting isn't how I thought it would be. I don't think I fit in."

"Oh." He slouched in his chair. I couldn't look at him. "You know, I was telling the guys at work about how you'd gotten a whole building in New York for free! Their kids are supposed to be so smart and all they do is go to college and ask for money all the time. They said I practically won the lottery!"

He'd already told me this story, but I felt so bad I didn't say anything.

"Well, I guess we shouldn't be surprised," he sighed. "If it sounds too good to be true, it probably is, right? Angela thinks I really dropped the ball, not helping you look at schools and all that."

"I don't need help, Dad. It's fine. I want to be in New York." I said this just to calm him down but when I heard it, I liked how it sounded. It was true.

"Okay," my dad nodded. "So, how's the job search going? Can you live in a squat and have a job or what?"

"Everyone works," I replied defensively. "I work at Donny's table on Sundays!"

"And you make what, thirty dollars? You can't live on that! You need a job."

I thought of Mitch, out all day in the world, and above it all when he was home, on the lofty third floor. That didn't look so bad. Especially now that it was winter and so cold, having someplace to go could be good.

"Get *any* job," my dad pleaded, "I can't give you money when you're not in school and you could be working. I'm married now. We both work."

"Okay." I felt my eyes well up. It's not that I wanted to be in Angela's place, living with my dad. I just felt . . . alone. He had a new life, my mom had a new life, and what did I have?

"You'll feel better. I know you will."

"Okay, I said I would!" I rubbed my eyes.

My dad sighed again. "I dropped the ball on you, didn't I, kiddo?"

"No, Dad, don't say that."

"When Angela said I should help you think about careers," he went on, "I said you weren't the kind of kid to take direction from your old man. You were more the type to give *me* directions."

It was true: I used to lecture him all the time. I told him not to eat meat, not to wear leather, not to buy records on major labels. Of course, he was a blue-collar guy who listened to opera and read history for fun—he liked independent thinking. He might argue with me a little, but he'd also tell anyone who'd listen how smart his kid was.

"It's not fair you only have one parent. I wish I'd met Angela when you were younger."

"*God*, Dad." Everything was hard enough without Angela hovering over us in judgment. "If anyone dropped the ball, it's my mom. What did *she* ever do?"

He hated it if I talked bad about my mom; I knew I was provoking him. I got up and went to the sink with my empty cup. But when he answered, he just sounded thoughtful: "When your mother left, she was the same age you are now."

I knew my mom had still lived with her parents when she'd met my dad, but I'd always pictured her as an adult. I could barely take care of myself; imagine having a baby. Horrifying.

"Did she want an abortion?" I leaned on the sink and looked out the window; it was starting to get light.

"No, but at first she thought we should have you adopted. You could have grown up with some nice stable family instead of moving all over creation with me. I talked her out of it. I was sure that once we had you, we'd be a happy little family. I was too stupid to see the whole picture." I knew what had happened after I was born: Things were fine when they still lived in Texas, but when my dad's job moved to Idaho she fell in with a wild crowd there. She wouldn't go with him and me when it was time to leave again. He thought if he went ahead without her, she would miss us and be sorry and come catch up.

"What didn't you see?"

"She didn't love me," he said. It had to be Angela's influence, him talking like this. "I was just a way out of Texas for her. She figured if I wanted the baby so bad she'd let me have it. You, I mean. Of course, I'm glad she did. But I don't know if it was the best thing for either of you two."

"You loved her and she didn't love you." I watched a car pull out of the condo's parking garage and slip into the dawn street.

My dad leaned forward over the table, fiddling with the salt shaker, so the morning light hit the bald spot at the top of his dark head. "So you get why Angela is so important. At forty-five? I'd almost given up." He smiled, trying to make it sound light. "I know you and Angela don't have a lot in common . . ."

"Angela's good for you, Dad," I said quickly. Now I felt bad for not making more of an effort with her. He was happy; I could see that. But I was already thinking in the past tense. I couldn't linger around any longer, hiding out in other people's lives.

I had forgotten how tough and powerful just seeing the Bakery made me feel: three stories of graffiti-covered bricks, my own piece of New York. The deadbolt turned and the heavy door croaked open just like it always had. In the icy, garbage-filled foyer, I felt hope.

But pushing through the blankets I'd hung in the first floor doorway, my optimism wavered. I stood staring around the room unable to fully take in what I was seeing. My bed, my rug, my trunk: gone. Right where my bed had been there was an oil drum with a chimney coming out of it—a homemade woodstove. Lazy Lorenzo had actually built a stove? I stepped back into the foyer and let the curtains swish back into place behind me, as if I had just made a mistake and walked into the wrong room. The house was silent and frozen.

I left my backpack in the foyer, locked the door behind me, and walked to Bedford Avenue. My dad had slipped me some cash. I'd get something to eat, calm down before I did anything.

The air was so cold it hurt to breathe. It was a relief to get to North 7th to the familiar L Café. The bells on the door jingled in an empty room when I pushed my way in. The girl behind the counter was alone. She leaned on her arms, playing with her long skinny braids.

"I remember you," she said when I ordered. "You're the girl with the Black Flag tattoo."

"That's me." I pulled back my sleeve to show her.

"My boyfriend's into hardcore. He said he'd never seen a chick with the Black Flag bars."

"They're great."

She shrugged. "That's what he says." She handed me my coffee and I stirred in milk and sugar.

"It's quiet here today," I said.

"Thank god! When the door opens it gets so cold in here!" She shivered dramatically. "Everyone's hunkered down at home."

"My home is colder than outside."

"You live in a loft? That sucks paying your own heat. I did that for a while. I was like, high ceilings, real pretty, whatever, get me back to a tiny warm apartment already, this sucks."

"What sucks more is living with assholes who throw your stuff out when you're gone a couple weeks." The coffee was producing a feeling of giddy power.

"No way!" The girl leaned over the counter. "They threw your stuff out?"

Now that I'd said it like that, it didn't sound right. Mitch wouldn't let anyone leave garbage in front of the building. Would Lorenzo really wait for trash night and sneak my stuff up and down the block? I couldn't picture that.

"Roommates are the worst," the girl said. "I lived with this chick who used to prance around in a towel whenever my boyfriend was visiting." She shimmied back behind the counter with her hands on her chest like Betty Boop.

A long-haired man came from the back with a tray of glasses. "Leslie," he said, "can you get those plates?"

I finished my sandwich and put a tip on the counter.

Back at the house, I looked around more carefully. Some of my tools were with Lorenzo's on the table I'd set up by the door. The old drill I'd bought from Veronica when she got herself a better one was out of its case. The battery was dead.

I climbed to the second floor. The winter sun glared through the west-facing windows. The light hit my unfinished mural, blurred with moisture in the cold. In a neat pile, centered at the base of the wall, were my art supplies. Watercolors, pencils, pastels.

"Skip," I breathed. He'd put them there. On the second floor—the art space.

"Sid, you're back." I jumped, startled. He was standing at his door in a puffy coat so huge he had to tilt his whole body back to see me from under the hood.

"You put this here?"

"I thought you'd need them," he said.

"But where . . . What happened . . . ?"

"Your things?" Skip moved past me quick and nervous, pointing up the stairs. He led the way to the third floor.

My velvet easy chair, the one I'd found in the trash and dragged three blocks, was in front of Mitch's woodstove.

Skip went into Jimmy's room at the front of the

building and I followed him. There was my mattress, my braided rug, my trunk. Garbage bags. I pulled one open. My quilt, T-shirts. I sank down on the mattress and Skip stood in the doorway, rubbing his hands together in his baggy fingerless gloves.

"Where's Jimmy?" I asked.

"He moved in with his girlfriend?" Skip prompted, like this was something I should remember.

"I . . . I just got back."

"You didn't talk to Mitch?"

I shook my head.

"Oh. Well, Eddie was going to move up here when Jimmy left. But . . ." He shrugged.

"But what?"

"Well, that was the plan. But Mitch said . . ." Skip paused, looking confused. "I mean, I thought you and Mitch had some . . . agreement."

"Agreement?"

"Don't ask me!" He threw up his hands. "I heard you and Lorenzo got in a fight, no one tells me anything! Mitch freaked out on those Spanish guys and Lorenzo went nuts. I thought they were going to kill each other! And you were gone and Mitch said to help him move your stuff up here, so we did."

"Like, for storage?"

Skip squinted. "He said you were going to live up here now?"

"When was this?"

"I don't know, before Christmas."

Probably the very day I had left, this had all been decided, while I sat around Baltimore worrying. Skip looked frustrated.

I asked, "Are you not happy about this?"

"It's done now." He crossed his arms around his big purple coat. "It's just, you know, we're cramped downstairs. I was going to make Eddie's room a kitchen and, I mean, Eddie's been here longer than you, no offense, but Mitch bit my head off and Eddie said he didn't want to move up here anyways, with Mitch all like that, and I just think it's the kind of decision we should make as a group."

"You're right. I totally agree. I'm so sorry. It's really embarrassing about . . . that Lorenzo . . . that me and Lorenzo . . ."

Skip's face squeezed up like he was scared I was going to cry. "We're your friends too. It's pretty nice up here, isn't it? It'll be easier to heat."

"Yeah," I agreed with my face in my hands. I didn't want to seem ungrateful. But the room was tiny, a fraction of the space I'd worked so hard on downstairs.

Skip kept talking while I pulled myself together. He told me everyone was gone. Eddie was at his sister's in Jersey, Mitch was somewhere, Lorenzo somewhere else. Mexico, Skip thought. Skip himself was on his way to see his grandma upstate. She was having trouble with her hip, and he went on and on until I was calm and could look at him and nod in the appropriate places. He felt guilty leaving me alone in the cold. Before he went, he brought up his space heater for me to borrow.

When he was gone, I walked around the quiet third floor. Mitch had a padlock on his bedroom door. The kitchen he'd set up in the open space was clean and organized. I could buy some tea at the store, things I could heat up on his hot plate.

I went back into Jimmy's room. Which I guess was now mine. Jimmy had left a Ramones poster which was curling up on one corner. I hadn't been able to put up posters downstairs on the crumbling brick. My crate of records and CDs was sitting by the doorway. I crouched down and flipped through them, soothed by the familiarity. If I put my mattress against the back wall, I'd be able to see out the windows while I lay in bed. Two big windows. I could see past the building across the street to the park and the highway, the sky through the bare tree branches.

On my way out to the store, I glanced at my mural again. It looked foreign to me, like someone else had started it. Someone much more punk and angry than I was now. If I painted a squatter mural today, it would be something more humble. A little bird, maybe. Quietly building a nest for herself out of other people's scraps.

VII

When I tried to leave the house after three days of blizzard, I found the front door blocked halfway to the lintel with a pile of snow. I felt like a bear emerging from hibernation into the harsh air. I used a piece of plywood to push enough snow aside so I could climb out. Next door, the sidewalk was salted and shoveled to make a pathway, but in front of the Bakery it was a glacier—no one had come or gone in days. My piss bucket was frozen solid and even with Skip's space heater on ten next to mine, I could still see my breath. I decided it was time to venture into the world and find someplace to take a bath. After a few phone calls and a train ride, I met Raven at an apartment where she was staying on Orchard Street.

"Whose place is this?" I asked as I walked in. Raven kissed me and her lip ring was warm on my cheek. She looked tiny wrapped in a rainbow kimono, with her dreads wound into a topknot like a samurai.

"My friend who's in Europe. She does, like, feminist burlesque, tassels on her tits and stuff. I met her down South train-hopping to gigs with these Vegas showgirl outfits in her backpack. She's *amazing*. Check out the bathroom." The apartment was like the Kasbah, everything red and gold. It was so overheated she had the windows cracked for air. Raven swept me through a hallway and pulled a feathered rope. Every inch of wall in the bathroom was covered in kitschy paint-by-numbers. Oriental scenes framed in gold.

Taking a bath after not washing for a week is an experience. I made the water scorching and scrubbed myself with a washcloth and I got out feeling loose and light, like I'd shed ten pounds.

Raven was on the couch drinking tea and reading the *Village Voice*. I stretched my pink feet in her lap.

When I told her about the fight with Lorenzo and the woodstove that had replaced me on our old floor, she didn't seem very surprised.

"You see the girls he likes? They weigh like seventy pounds and wear pink lipstick! And your room upstairs sounds way better. So you win." She moved my feet so she could pour more tea from a pot shaped like a pagoda. "Want honey?"

My feelings were hurt. She just saw the story as me being in love with Lorenzo and that excused his meanness? Raven's romances were always weird and secret. She'd been sneaking around all summer with this bi-curious fashion model who lived with her boyfriend; and there was a guy at work, too; and an older artist she'd go see uptown who didn't want his kids to know about her. I took the tea and looked around the room all sulky.

"I thought you were against owning stuff, doesn't all this clutter annoy you?"

"I don't dislike *other* people's stuff," Raven said. "I just think squatters shouldn't have a lot of things. Once you have stuff, you want to protect it and you aren't ready for action and focused on the communal good."

"Speaking of having stuff," I picked up the *Voice* and turned to the back, "I need a job. What do you think I'm good at?"

"Construction?"

"Some foreman is going to hire me?"

"Can you drive? I know a pot dealer who needs help with deliveries."

"Wait, check this out. *Clerk for dominatrix dungeon and fetish store. Must be sex positive and fantastic on the phone.*"

"They'll love you! Call!" Raven grabbed her friend's bright-red phone and set it in front of me.

I knew I was good on the phone. I had learned to overcome shyness by copying the way the waitresses at the diner by my high school talked. They called everyone *Hon* and were real bossy. So when I got the lady from the dungeon on the line, I pitched my voice low and said, "Well, I just thought this job sounds like a real hoot."

Raven clapped a hand over her mouth. The lady on the phone asked what kind of experience I had.

"Since I moved to New York I've been selling records at punk shows," I responded. She asked if I could come in for an interview that afternoon.

"Let's get you dressed!" Raven cried, flipping open

a beaded curtain that led to a bedroom. "You can't go dressed like a boy."

I looked in the mirror. Levi's. Bullet belt. Band T-shirt over thermal. In the warm apartment I wasn't wearing my stained and torn-up old hoodie or scuffed combat boots, but they were part of my usual uniform too.

"Squatters should have no gender," I said.

Raven dug through the closet. "Whatever, if I had your boobs I'd show 'em off." She shook a dress at me. "Check out this blue, it'd match your eyes."

"No skirts!" I was horrified. "I'll look like a transvestite!"

Raven put the dress back in the closet and scrutinized me in the mirror. "Maybe, like, hot butch dyke is the direction to go?"

"I wish I was gay. Lesbians love big girls."

"Totally. You'd be an amazing lesbian. Maybe she's got a leather vest or something." Raven continued digging through the closet. She pulled out a shiny bright-orange shirt. "Ooo, this'd work, it's stretchy."

"It won't fit," I said, but Raven insisted, so I left my undershirt over my bra and tugged at the vintage polyester in the mirror.

"Nice! Cleavage!" Raven rolled the sleeves to my elbows and we considered me in the mirror. I wasn't used to showing skin. It did look more sophisticated than my band T-shirt. The bold color was something the brassy girl I'd just played on the phone might wear.

"Lipstick!" Raven announced. She tied a scarf around

my hair too. I'd bleached it over the summer when it was as short as Raven's. Now it was grown out to shoulder length with dark roots. At least it was clean from my bath. I liked how my face looked framed by the scarf, with the lipstick and powder and the fake fur coat Raven insisted I wear.

I took the subway uptown. I switched at West 4th Street and caught the C to Port Authority. The dungeon was on the far West Side. I breathed the Ninth Avenue air deep into my lungs. It was damp and raw today, not icy like it had been. Taxicabs and discarded Christmas trees and gray snow piles. I took big swinging steps, trying to stay in the character of the girl on the phone. The lipstick made a bright reflection in the storefront windows as I walked by. It was fun. Maybe I'd buy my own lipstick if I got the job. Maybe I'd get a little vintage handbag like a riot grrrl.

The lady in charge of the dungeon, Kathy, had a pile of witchy gray hair in a complicated 'do and wore heels and a skirt belted high on her waist. I felt underdressed even in my getup. But I managed to answer her questions without making an ass of myself. She said girls needed to be tough to work there and she liked my sass and hired me on the spot. Weekday afternoons I would be receptionist and clerk, ringing up sales of dildos and scheduling appointments for whippings. It all sounded perfectly normal when Kathy explained it in her businesslike way.

It was a new world, commuting with the rest of Brooklyn into the city, hurrying along 42nd Street with somewhere to go. I sat at an impressive-looking oak desk and pretended I knew what I was talking about. Within a few days, I saw that the dungeon wasn't as subversive a place as I thought it would be. The dominatrixes acted like spoiled sorority girls. One of them was in a snit on Valentine's Day because her boyfriend had given her carnations instead of roses. I couldn't believe she was serious, I'd thought when I finished sixth grade I'd never have to hear about Valentine's Day again.

"Oh my god, what a fat book!" Mistress Laure teetered over me one afternoon, engulfing me with the smell of her jasmine perfume. She had a military cap over her long red hair. "What is it?"

It was a quiet afternoon. I showed her the cover. "*Bleak House*?" she breathed. "That looks so *old*! What's it about?"

"There're these orphans . . ."

Kathy came clicking down the hallway in a serious way and we both turned.

"He still in there?" Laure asked her. A client had come in awhile ago for the other dominatrix, Alison. Laure didn't have anyone for another hour.

"Now he's crying." Kathy threw her hands in the air.

"What's going on?" I asked.

"That cop, he put on a full-body cat suit and then locked himself in the bathroom. She can't budge him," Laure explained. She clearly loved that Alison was flailing; the two of them didn't get along at all. Alison liked to flaunt that she had a fiancé, which upset Laure who was single and tragic about it.

"He's a cop?" I asked. I remembered the guy. He'd had a mustache, but he wasn't wearing a uniform.

"Oh, sure, it's all cops and Wall Street guys," Laure said. "It's the pressure, they need to feel helpless to relax."

"I thought I'd give Alison some space." Kathy pursed her lips. "I was making her nervous. Maybe . . . Laure, sweetie, could you . . . ?"

Laure inspected a glossy purple fingernail with elaborate nonchalance.

"Would you have a glance in there?"

"Oh, you want me to fix it?" Laure stretched slowly and let her satin robe slither to the floor, exposing her bodice and buckled leather shorts. She spun on a heel and stalked down the hallway.

A minute later Alison came steaming down the hall in a huff. "I would have gotten him out!" she cried to Kathy. "Why does that—"

"Get back in there," Kathy ordered, hands on her hips, "and watch what Laure does. You might learn something."

Alison stormed off and Kathy sank into the chair next to me, kicking off her heels. "You see why I have to wear these?" she said, wiggling her toes.

"So you're taller than the girls?"

"Of course there's an argument that high heels are

bondage, to make a woman unable to flee. So she has to be defended by a man," Kathy said. I almost laughed, it sounded like she was paraphrasing Crass lyrics. She reached for Laure's discarded kimono and folded it. "But being tall conveys authority. Sometimes you just have to use what works."

I didn't tell Kathy that I thought it was important to live by your principles, no matter what. What would I back up my ideas with, quotes from *Bikini Kill* zines? I'd only expose my lack of education. I also didn't ask how Laure had coaxed the cop out of the bathroom, though I was dying to know.

"It's all cops and Wall Street guys," I explained to Veronica, when we met after work for a drink at International Bar where they didn't ID. I was celebrating my first paycheck, my first lipstick, my new beeper. All winter no one could have reached me except by letter or carrier pigeon. I felt like I was back in the land of the living.

"Cops?" Veronica laughed. "That's crazy! Next time you're at an eviction, you'll be all like, *Not so fast there, buster!*"

I snorted into the martini I'd ordered to be fancy. "*I know you, Mr. Cat-Suit Man!*"

"When clients are assholes to us," Veronica said, "my boss'll paint curse words on the walls before we cover them up!" She was working uptown now, painting a pristine ten-room apartment a slightly-more-subtle shade of beige.

We had a second drink. I didn't tell Veronica what had happened with Lorenzo. Even Raven hadn't been sympathetic, and I didn't want to hear Veronica say that I talked about him too much. Instead, I told her about Mistress Laure eating one of Mistress Alison's cupcakes and getting her hair pulled before Kathy intervened.

We joked about girl fights all the way back to Veronica's, where she'd invited me to take a shower without making me ask. I always kept a towel in my messenger bag in case of unexpected shower opportunities. It was really hard to stay clean enough for a job. I had looked into joining a gym near work so I could shower there, but between that and subway tokens and buying lunch in Midtown, I'd have nothing left over. Having a job was expensive. But I liked it so far.

A couple nights later Mitch tapped on my bedroom door. "You hungry?"

"Um, I don't know . . ." I'd been keeping to my new room since Mitch got back a couple days before. I was afraid he would really rub it in—how stupid I'd been to trust Lorenzo and how he'd tried to warn me.

"You don't know if you're hungry? Well, I made soup. It's vegetarian. Come on."

I would have preferred to stay hidden in my room where I wasn't bothering anyone, but I didn't want to offend Mitch so I followed him to the kitchen.

"Did you use the kitchen while I was gone?" He spoke with his back to me, stirring a steaming pot.

I chewed on my lip. Had I left something out of place? "Just, like, to make tea . . ."

He glanced over his shoulder. "I don't mind, as long as you clean up." In addition to the hot plate, he had a little fridge and a sink set into the counter. He pointed to the water jug over the old sink that drained into a bucket; he used it to wash dishes. "If the waste water gets full, just throw it in the gutter when you go to the hydrant. Anyone been using the woodstove?"

"No. No one's been up here except me." I sat at the table and fiddled with one of the two spoons he'd put out already. "Lorenzo has his stove going downstairs now, so . . . I guess they all hang out there."

"The Three fucking Stooges," Mitch smirked. "They all hate me now." He set two bowls on the table and sat down.

"I haven't really seen anyone since I moved up here." I blew on my spoon to cool my soup down. When I looked up, Mitch was watching me.

"That okay?" he asked, his bruised-looking blue eyes showing actual concern.

"Yeah . . ." I put down my spoon. "I should . . . I should thank you."

"You like it?"

"I do! It's great, it was so nice of you, I didn't expect—"

"It's not a big deal."

"It is, though! I didn't know what I was going to do."

He swallowed. "Well, I usually make it vegetarian even when I'm alone. I think it needs salt, though, doesn't it?"

"Salt?"

He got up and grabbed the blue box from the counter. "No?"

"It's really good," I mumbled. "What's in it?"

"What *isn't* in Camp Soup!" Mitch smiled. I'd never seen him so relaxed. "My dad made it like this when we were in the woods, it all goes in one pot. Tortellini, potatoes, red pepper . . ."

"Where did you camp?"

"We have this cabin up in Maine. Actually, it's mine now. It's on this little island you get to by motorboat. Totally off the grid."

"Sounds lonely."

"Nah, it's great! You know what's funny is, the town where you get groceries and stuff is called Brooklin. Brooklin, Maine. That's why I wanted to live out here, I guess, when I came to New York. Kinda sentimental, I guess . . . You been to Maine?"

"I went to New Hampshire once."

"Where?"

"Portsmouth. My mom lives there. She works at the Home Depot."

"No shit! What department?"

I was hitting the jackpot here, New England and building supplies. I'd always found Mitch hard to talk to but clearly I'd just never tried the right subjects.

"Paint," I replied. I never talked about my mom. I had only gone to visit because my dad made me. I'd been so miserable I ran away from Portsmouth after two

days. The police had picked me up on the highway trying to hitchhike home.

"Someday I'm gonna go live in Maine," Mitch said.
"Grow my own food, shoot stuff, be totally self-sufficient."

He showed me a catalog from an Amish company
that made tools for people who lived without electricity.
He had things circled that he was saving up for. A washing machine you cranked by hand; a fridge that ran on
propane. I wanted to tease him for being a hippie, but
I didn't dare. He could still be a loose cannon. Like the
next day when I mentioned I was going to meet Raven
at Food Not Bombs and his face got sour and he started
muttering about punk idiots with their lame-ass causes.

And it was touch and go with the boom box in the
kitchen. While I was cleaning up one night, I put on the
new Sleater-Kinney and he charged out of his room with
his face scrunched like he was having a stroke. "That
sounds like a cat in heat!" he yelled. But I discovered
that he could tolerate Jawbreaker and Lungfish. Green
Day was another story. *Dookie* turned him into a pussy-
cat; he'd bop his head and sing along in a surprisingly
pretty falsetto.

"You're lookin' at a reformed choir boy over here!" he
said proudly, to my raised eyebrows.

I didn't set eyes on Lorenzo for another week. Then one
night I was coming in the house after work and Lorenzo
must have been on his way out. He was in the entrance to
the first floor holding back the blanket curtains. He was

only a few feet from me with his familiar black dreads and smooth dark skin. He looked tan and healthy. He was wearing a new coat too. He'd been with his family in Mexico. He turned back into his room like he hadn't seen me, and I was startled to find myself suddenly on the third floor, panting, with a hand clutched over my heart. My favorite CD was playing in the lamp-lit kitchen.

"*Sometimes I give myself the creeps . . .*" Mitch sang along with Billie Joe while he stirred a pot on the hot plate, his face pink in the steam. "Hey," he called over his shoulder, "you eat?"

VIII

My new beeper lit up: *911*. Emergency? Then Veronica's number. It was the first Sunday in March and sunlight poured into the tall windows on the third-floor kitchen like winter was ready to be over. What kind of emergency could Veronica have? I had to make coffee before I went to the corner to make a phone call, I was groggy from sleeping late.

Boots hammered up the stairs and Lorenzo appeared, a watch cap over his dreads. He started for my room and then noticed me standing by the hot plate.

"Hey," I said. We hadn't spoken since our fight. Mitch stepped to the doorway of his room, thinking I'd spoken to him, and stiffened when he saw Lorenzo.

"Rot-Squat," Lorenzo gasped. "On fire!"

"Oh no! What's the—"

"S'all I know. I just talk to Diego, we got cut off." Lorenzo was already retreating. "Goin' over there."

"My friend Raven's house," I explained to Mitch, almost apologetically, thinking of his reaction the last time I'd mentioned her. I ran to my room for my coat. When I came out, Mitch was at the top of the stairs, his hood pulled up.

"I'm coming with," he said.

We couldn't get anywhere near Rot-Squat. A crowd hovered around the corner and Avenue B was entirely blocked by police barricades, fire trucks, officers. I could see Rot-Squat from the corner, tall and intact in the middle of the block where it belonged. It hadn't burned down, but there was black soot scorched into the façade.

On the corner I saw Lee, someone I knew from Rot-Squat. I had even been in his room that one time when he and his friends were on pills. He was standing with a bunch of kids I recognized from 5th Street Squat. "Is everyone okay?" I asked him.

"This is total bullshit!" he exploded. He glanced up and down at Mitch, like he was wondering who my football player pal was. "There was hardly any fire! It was just in Billy's space and that's it!"

"And now what? Where is everyone?"

"They all left the building," he said. "The smoke and all. The fire department's not letting anyone back in."

One of the 5th Street squatters, a tall guy with earplugs, raised his voice as a crew-cut man with an *Office of Emergency Management* jacket passed: "It's these fuckin' goons of Giuliani's."

A skinny kid with a pit bull ran up to join us, breathing hard in the cold air. "They're calling the building condemned!"

"Shit," Earplugs clicked his tongue piercing against

his teeth, "that's why they got HPD here, you see that? That's not for a fire."

"Condemned?" Lee growled. "That's a total joke!"

"Yeah, the place next door has no roof, check it out!" Earplugs pointed. "It's been condemned for years! Never been any fuckin' emergency."

"Thirteenth Street all over again," I said. Everyone in the neighborhood remembered the tanks that had evicted those squats, it was just a few years ago.

"How'd the fire start?" Mitch broke in, dropping his r's, showing his Boston. Everyone looked at him. Even if I felt like introducing him, I couldn't, because I didn't know all these kids' names.

"Fuckin' Billy." Lee looked down over his thin nose and spoke to me as if I was the one who'd asked. "Stupid hippie. He went out and left his space heater on. Bad cord or something."

"Were you inside?" I asked him.

"I don't live there anymore. I'm working on a space at 5th Street."

"Sid!" The ragged yell made us all turn. Raven leaned over the barricade, wrapped in a gray Red Cross blanket like it was a cape. I ran to hug her with the blue police barricade squeezed between us. She was on the side where only block residents were allowed. Behind her, closer to Rot-Squat, I could see familiar faces: Stumps yelling at an emergency worker, his round face red in the cold; Abby, with her blond hair sticking out from under a Red Cross blanket.

"Where's your coat?" I asked Raven, rubbing her shoulders.

"It was so beautiful out!" she cried. "We were at Sidewalk!" They all went every day for the $2.99 breakfast and the running water and the bathroom. You could set your watch by them hurrying across the park with sleep in their eyes, boots unlaced and coats flapping, toothbrushes in their pockets, at five minutes to two, when the special ended. "I had my camera with me at least!" She flashed me her big old Nikon, hidden under the blanket. "I got *crazy* pictures. Will you find me more film? I want to document everything; this is totally illegal. Did you hear they condemned the building?" Her voice broke with emotion. "I can't get more film, if I leave the block they won't let me back here!"

"I'll get it, I'll be right back. Take my hat, I have a hood." I pulled the wool over her ears and she shut her eyes for a moment before she dashed back into the fray.

Going to the bodega for film gave me a purpose. Mitch shadowed me like a bodyguard, like he was relieved to have something useful to do too. After we delivered it to Raven, we stood around in little gangs of neighborhood squatters and residents, everyone upset, irate, spreading rumors and speculating. At first I worried Mitch would say something obnoxious to the squatters I talked to, or the girls I knew from Food Not Bombs, or the hardcore dudes from ABC. But he kept his mouth shut. Actually, I liked having him around. I didn't have to impress or entertain him. And on my own, I might have felt weird hanging around so long, like an outsider. But I really wanted to stay. I wanted to be here and witness what happened. I saw Lorenzo pass with some girls I didn't know. I spotted Veronica from a distance with a bunch of her intimidating housemates. She looked for a second like she was going to come over until she saw who I was with. Mitch had been so awful the time she met him at our house. She just waved.

The fire had been out for hours. Everyone on the street pointed out that officers without hard hats or gear were going in and out of Rot-Squat, so the building had to be safe. The Rot-Squatters, caged with barricades on the sidewalk opposite their house, begged to be let back inside. But they were ignored.

After dark, a wrecking crane appeared on the block, and word went around: now that the building was condemned, Giuliani had ordered it demolished immediately. Removing squatters from a building was dangerous and expensive. They were like fleas, the way they held on, got in all the cracks. The Rot-Squatters were out now and Giuliani was too smart to miss his chance. A lawyer who was squatter-friendly was already on site, discussing what would happen in the morning. She would try to get a stay of demolition first thing.

It had been dark for hours, it was freezing, and the police insisted nothing else was happening tonight. Raven and Abby left the barricaded street a bit after eight. I hugged them together, our heads in a huddle. Abby was almost hysterical, talking fast, incoherent. Raven was quiet and dull. They were going to stay with a friend at C-Squat and I watched them walk down the street leaning on each other like old ladies. I turned, looking for Mitch, who I'd gotten so used to as my shadow all day. He was gone. I felt a surge of panic, like I'd lost my wallet. I wasn't surprised that he'd gotten bored and walked off. But I was surprised by how hurt I felt that he hadn't said goodbye.

Lee and his friends from 5th Street leaned against a building at the end of the block under a streetlamp and I meandered over near them. I didn't have the energy to think of anything to say. I just sat on a stoop nearby and rested my head in my hands.

"Here."

I looked up. Mitch held a blue-and-white deli cup. "Take it."

"For me?" The cup was warm through my gloves.

He sat next to me. "Got some sandwiches." He opened a white bag and held out a foil-wrapped package, but I just stared at it. He hadn't asked me for money or anything.

"You don' want it?" he asked.

"Are you sure? Yes, thank you!" I hadn't realized how hungry I was. I unwrapped it and took a ravenous bite. Egg and cheese on a warm roll.

"Why Miss Sidney!" I smelled the jasmine perfume before I saw her looming over me. Laure extended an elegant gloved hand to Mitch like he was my date at a cocktail party. "Hello, I work with Sid. And you are . . . ?"

"This is Mitch," I managed. I didn't want to be outed as a squatter to anyone from work, or seen to know this ditzy sorority girl by the guys from 5th Street, or by Mitch for that matter. I took a big gulp of coffee to get the sandwich down and burned my mouth.

Laure took in the 5th Street kids with their piercings, pit bulls, and patches, and gave a shriek, gloved hand flying to her mouth. "Oh gosh, you didn't *live* there, did you?"

"No, no," I said, "our friends . . . I mean . . ." Were the 5th Street guys listening? Wondering why I was claiming Rot-Squat as my friends? I took a bite of sandwich to shut myself up.

Mitch stepped in: "We figured people should stick around, you know. Keep an eye on what happens."

"Of course! The poor things, what the city is doing is out-*ra*-geous!" Laure crouched down next to me on her long legs. "My sister's apartment is right next door." She pointed to a tenement that was separated from Rot-Squat only by the drooping derelict building that Earplugs had said had no roof. "She told me the people at the squat were so nice, not what you'd—" She stopped herself with a twitter. "You have to meet my sister." She waved, and a shorter, blonder version of Laure trotted over in heeled boots.

"It's *too* awful." The sister crouched next to Laure. "Is there anything we can do to help?" They looked up at us, like we were in charge. Mitch flicked an amused smile at me over his coffee cup and I relaxed a little.

"You live in that building there?" Mitch pointed. The girls nodded in unison.

He stood to get a better view, craning his neck at the row of buildings. It looked as if their apartment building and Rot-Squat were holding up the sagging condemned building between them like a drunken friend. Mitch peered down at me now, studying my face like he had the buildings. "Their roofs are all connected," he said.

I stood up. "Oh wow. So if we can get in one . . ."

"You got roof access at your place?" he asked the girls.

They nodded.

To me he said, "Those kids'll need their stuff outta there, if the city's demolishing it tomorrow."

I stared at him, my mind reeling with the idea. "Could we really get in?" I asked. But I already trusted him. If anyone could pull it off, Mitch could.

"Why not?" His eyes sparkled. I stepped over to the 5th Street kids and told them our plan.

"But the cops aren't letting anyone on the block," Earplugs gestured at the checkpoint.

Lee smacked him on the arm. "That's what she's saying, doofus! She's saying she knows someone on the block!"

"So we can get past the cops?" the skinny pit bull kid jumped in. "Let's go!"

I wondered if Lorenzo was around still. He was the first person I thought of, I wanted him to see me doing this.

Laure and her sister hooked arms and led the way to where the police were checking IDs like it was East Berlin. Mitch took my arm and whispered, "Pretend we're a couple."

"Driver's license," the cop said as we approached.

Laure's sister handed hers over, tapping the address. "I live right there at 325. See? And this is my sister and our friends from college who came to stay with us from . . ." she glanced at my license and read, "Connecticut."

At the same moment Laure, glancing at Mitch's, said, "Massachusetts."

The cop looked us over. It was dark. I had my hood pulled up so you couldn't see my streaked hair or all my silver earrings. Mitch's Carhartt jacket was clean and new, not ripped and patched like a squatter's. We were waved through. We hurried past and heard his tone change for the group behind us. "And where do you think you're going?" he barked. Lee gave me a hopeless shrug from the wrong side of the barricades; they weren't getting by.

Laure's sister didn't have to use her key to get into her building, her neighbors were clustered in the lobby with the door open. I had the idea that anyone who paid rent in New York had to be yuppie scum, but there were some guys here who wouldn't look out of place at a hardcore show, a black guy with long gray dreads in a karate outfit, a Latina grandma offering everyone tamales, and an Asian goth girl I'd seen around the neighborhood. We made our way upstairs to the top floor, trading checkpoint horror stories with everyone.

From the warm apartment, I used the phone to call Raven at C-Squat. "We're on the block!" I whispered, like the cops down in the street might hear me.

"Holy crap!" she yelled. The room she was in was full of voices. "You think you can get into Rot-Squat?"

"I don't know, we're going to try," I said. "Find out what people want out of there, so we get the right stuff."

I sat by the phone writing notes, while Raven tracked people down at other squats and bars and friends' houses and called me over and over. I took notes carefully like I was really going to pull this off. Twenty-four people had lived at Rot-Squat but she couldn't find them all. Mitch borrowed flashlights from neighbors and went up to the roof to plan our route. Laure and her sister gave us tea and hot soup and then they put on a movie in the bedroom.

I was finished with my calls and dozing on an antique velvet couch with an orange cat purring on my belly when Mitch woke me up.

"Time to go," he said.

IX

From the roof, Avenue B looked like a prison yard in a movie, overlit by police spotlights brought in on trucks. The officers at the intersections had settled into their warm cars. Everyone on the block was inside, drapes and blinds pulled tight against the cold.

The roof of the building we were standing on was edged by a waist-high wall. Below us was the derelict building. Beyond that, Rot-Squat was taller, the same height as the apartment building where we stood. It was completely black in the dark, the police had cut the electricity.

Mitch pointed out how we were going to rappel down to the roof next door using this skinny-looking rope he'd found and secured to a pipe.

"Rappel?" I squinted over the ledge but the roof next door was only a vague spot in the shadows. From the ground, the roofs had looked closer together. "I thought the roof was all full of holes. They said that's why it was never squatted."

"Yeah, stay close to the edge till we see what's what," Mitch said, his breath pluming white in the cold. He climbed onto the ledge and tried to steady his feet against the building, holding the rope like a mountain climber. But it didn't work like that, he fell fast with a thud, the thin rope pulling taut but doing little to slow him down.

"You okay?" I gripped the side of the building, my armpits suddenly damp with sweat.

"Yeah, yeah."

I could just see the white of his face. I couldn't do it. Why had I called around like an idiot, and told all those people I was going to do this? That part had been fun, I hadn't been thinking about this. I stalled, testing the knot on the rope.

"Come on!" Mitch hissed at me. He held out his arms. "Here, I'll catch you!"

The idea was so ridiculous it made me annoyed. I'd crush him, obviously. "Get out of the way!" I hissed back. I wrapped the rope around my hands and stepped over the edge, pulling it taut and resting my feet against the side of the building. But with my gloves the rope had no way to move, so then I was stuck. I pulled, trying to ease the rope, and it broke loose. I fell and landed on my back.

"Crap." I held up the rope, looking up at Mitch.

"Never mind. You okay?" He put out a hand like he wanted to help me up, but I ignored it and got up on my own.

I followed Mitch to the middle of the roof where there was a way down. My foot sank into rotten wood and I stumbled. Mitch immediately reached for my arm.

I shouldn't have stalled on the roof ledge, now he was going to treat me like a girl. We headed down a shaky pigeon-shit ladder. It stank inside, even frozen. Kids with apartments on the south side of Rot-Squat tossed their garbage in here through the airshafts. Raven had told me that on the third floor the fire escape from Rot-Squat got close enough to a window in this building that people had climbed over. So we moved toward the street side of the building. The police spotlights poured through the gaping window holes. Keeping out of view, we crawled to a window.

Over the sill we could see the fire escape wasn't far, but it was very exposed. "How're we going to get the window open?" I asked. "The spotlight'll be right on us."

"You been arrested for trespassing?" Mitch's voice took on his old tough-guy swagger. His face was white-washed in the bright light. "It's not so bad. You get out in one night. In Boston at least. You meet some kooks in there, I'll tell you that."

"Getting arrested in Boston isn't exactly in the plan here," I said. This was no time to show off. "The cops might not be so nice in a real city."

Mitch looked out the window considering. Then he said quieter, "Let's see if we can get in the back."

We crouch-walked out of the bright room. He had backed down so fast it made me feel bad for being sarcastic. To be nice I asked, "So you've done this before, I take it?"

"One time I got stuck for a whole day in a building

I broke into. These thugs who were guarding the place were looking for me."

"That's scary."

He gave a shrug. "They couldn't find me. I always liked empty buildings. The quiet. I'd get pissed off at my dad, you know. Run off. I was into, like, guys who survived in the wild with nothing, you know? Did you read Jack London?"

"So squatting was the wild for you."

"I didn't even know it was called squatting. I'd just crash in a place a day or two till I felt like going home . . . Watch your step here, want my arm?"

On the back of the second floor we found a window that wasn't boarded up. We peered down on a yard that was shared with Rot-Squat next door. There was a ladder leading from the yard up into the squat, just a few feet from where we were. Mitch frowned at it. Who would be going into Rot-Squat with a ladder? The police? Looters? Well, we had come this far and hadn't found another way in. I swung a leg over the sill.

"Hey, wait," Mitch said in surprise.

I ignored him and fumbled until I hit a tiny ledge on the outside of the building. I clung to bricks and a drainpipe and concentrated on easing myself along the building toward the ladder. I was only one story off the ground. I told myself it wasn't much farther than the fall to the roof upstairs. I reached my left leg out and got the edge of the ladder, but in the dark I misjudged and pulled it off balance. The ladder tipped toward me and

I braced myself, waiting for it to crash into me. But it caught on the window frame in Rot-Squat and stopped.

"Careful!" Mitch hissed.

Someone from inside Rot Squat righted the ladder and leaned out. A flashlight shone in my face, blinding me, and I held fast to the drainpipe with my eyes squeezed tight.

A familiar, nasal voice cried, "Aww, *shit*, squatters!" He turned the light under his chin to make a demon face, catching the metal stud in his eyebrow, the gold teeth.

"Stumps! You scared the crap out of me!"

"Get the fuck in here, you crazy kid!" He held the ladder steady and I climbed onto it and over the window frame. I found myself in his bedroom. There was a mattress, TV, backpacks open on the bed.

"How'd you get in?" I asked while Stumps held the ladder for Mitch.

"The super next door loaned me this ladder, I hook him up," he grinned. Of course: Stumps sold dust and weed to everyone on the block.

"Welcome to the last night of Rot-Squat!" Stumps greeted Mitch. "How'd you guys get on the block?"

"We know this girl—" I started, but Mitch snorted through his teeth and said, "Maybe 'cause we don't look like scumbags." He sounded very Boston meathead. I was embarrassed.

Stumps cocked his head at Mitch like he was amused.

Mitch looked around. "There's no fire damage in here!"

"Yeah, right?" Stumps pointed out of his bedroom door to the front of the building. "I'm right behind Billy's room, it's right up there! These buildings are *solid*! His room's wet from the hoses and stuff but in here it just stinks."

"It sure does," I agreed. The smoke smell was nauseating. I pulled my scarf up to cover my nose.

"Fuckin' Giuliani." Stumps kicked his mattress in frustration. "Condemn *his* ass."

I pulled my notes out of my pocket. Raven wanted the cash under her mattress and her binder of negatives. Another girl wanted her passport which I would find hidden between books in her room somewhere on the third floor. The guy in the attic wanted his pill stash. It had been so much effort just to get in here, and our job hadn't even started.

"You been busy, yo!" Stumps whistled, looking at my notes. "I'll come find you guys when I get done here."

Mitch and I went out to the wide hallway. There were four apartments on the floor surrounding a staircase with no railing.

"Where do we even start?" I said. "Should we go to the top or . . ."

Mitch strode to the rear apartment next to Stumps and slammed his boot near the lock. The door flew open and a white cat dashed past us and up the stairs. I stood frozen a moment, waiting to hear if the noise brought cops. But the building was quiet. This must be Eli and Lydia's space; they'd asked me to let Iggy the cat out.

They said he'd be able to find his way out of the building from upstairs.

I followed Mitch inside and consulted my list. Like Raven, they'd been out when the fire started. They wanted their winter coats, Eli's collection of *Star Wars* figures, and Lydia's jewelry box.

Mitch found the shelf before I did. "He collects *toys*?" he scoffed, picking up a Han Solo, still in the box.

"They're valuable, I guess."

"They're *use*less!"

"They must be sentimental or something." I found a duffel bag full of dirty laundry and emptied it on the bed. Mitch's broad back blocked the shelf. "Let me in here," I said.

"This is bullshit." He shook his head. "We can't take every little thing."

"He didn't *ask* for every little thing! He asked for *these*, get out of my way!"

Mitch stepped aside and watched me cram the figures in the duffel bag. I shoved the two warmest-looking coats from hooks on the wall on top of them. I hoped they were the right ones. I found the jewelry box. It made me want to cry. What would I want, if I could only ask for a couple of my things? What about all their clothes, books . . . ? What were they forgetting about? I scanned a shelf: did they have a photo album, maybe? But the duffel bag was already full and heavy on my shoulder.

Mitch reached for it. "Here, let me."

"I got it." I held the strap tightly, still annoyed at

him. This was my moment to help Rot-Squat, to do my part for these people because I believed in their rights and what they had built here. It could be so amazing to be here if only I was with someone else, someone who actually belonged here and got it, instead of Mitch who was such an outsider. And who reminded me that I was too.

"Come on," he said, still reaching for the bag.

"I *said* I *got* it!" I swatted his hand away, overcome with frustration. "Stop treating me like a *girl!*"

He stepped back, looking startled.

"We have a lot of work to do!" I said. "If you're going to be a jerk then just go home!"

"What? What the hell did I do?"

"You're always judging everyone!"

I pushed past him and up the dark stairs to the third floor, breathing the evil smoke smell. I dropped the duffel bag in the hallway by Abby's open door. She'd told me how she had been in the building when it filled with smoke, running around the room like a trapped rat, unable to decide what to take, until Stumps had come in and pulled her down the stairs through smoke so thick they couldn't see a foot in front of them. I thought of the staircase. It had no railing, no risers. I shuddered. They knew the building well enough to make it out blind, but she swore that if Stumps hadn't come for her, she would have been too panicked to go down, not knowing if she was walking into flames or not.

Mitch entered the room behind me. "What're we looking for here?"

I checked my notes. "Quilt her grandma made, clothes. That okay with you?"

"Jeez, I'm sorry, all right?"

He helped me pile things up on the quilt. It was very dark, even with the flashlights we'd borrowed next door, and we were in a hurry, so our choices felt heartbreakingly random. Mitch rolled the quilt into a bundle and secured it with two studded belts. He put it in the hall with the duffel bag.

Apartment after apartment: we found Raven's negatives and cash; a guy's PlayStation; another guy's guitar. Someone I didn't know who lived on the fourth floor wanted his tools. His apartment was tidy and sparse.

Mitch ran a finger over the edge of the loft bed. "Dovetail joints," he said. The guy had saws and drills and metal toolboxes and a workbench with a neat row of chisels wrapped in leather to protect their blades. We put them in the case of a drill that Mitch said was expensive, but that was all we could take; everything was so heavy.

Stumps joined us and helped us carry all the bags we'd filled to apartments on the south side of the building, where we threw it all through the airshaft into the condemned building next door. The bags landed on piles of garbage in the dark. We'd go next door and find them all after this. Bag by bag, floor by floor, we worked our way down. Our arms got tired and weak and we moved slow, half asleep. We almost lost the guitar into the airshaft and I was so upset I had to go sit with my back against the wall, trembling, while Stumps and

Mitch finished. That's why I heard the noise downstairs. "Shhh!" I hissed at them.

From the second-floor hallway we could feel the air from the street; the front door had been opened. There were voices. Cops. Stumps hoisted the last pack and dashed into his room and we followed. Mitch shut and locked the apartment door behind us. I went first down the ladder, then Mitch, then Stumps. From the ground of the narrow concrete airshaft we moved the ladder a couple feet over so it led into the derelict building.

I was on my way up when someone opened a door below us. I scrambled through the window and ducked like I was taking cover from firefight in a movie.

The ladder rattled in the window and Mitch joined me. "It's okay, the guy next door," he whispered.

Stumps climbed through the window after him, and then leaned out the window and saluted. "Jose's gotta put the ladder away," he told us, "so he don't get in trouble. He's scared of the owner. But we can go out the way you guys came in, right?"

Stumps started toward the middle of the building, so he didn't see Mitch chewing his lip. With our rope to Laure's roof broken, we didn't exactly have a plan.

We tiptoed through the dark building and collected the bags and bundles we'd tossed down the airshaft. We could peek into the hallways in Rot-Squat here and there through the windowless holes in the air shaft, and we couldn't see any activity inside yet. We still had some time before it was light out. We struggled with our treasures, slowly making it to the rickety, half-eroded ladder. I made my way up the ladder onto the roof of the derelict building. Once on the roof I lay on my belly, the cold numbing my whole front, and reached down while Mitch and Stumps handed things up to me. The sky was pink now, getting lighter by the second. It was going to be a sunny day.

Once it was all on the roof, we had to get it to the apartment building next door. Some of the lighter things like duffel bags we could throw up that high. But most of the stuff was too heavy. I was so exhausted my arms were numb and useless.

Mitch studied the apartment building and said, "I thought the noise would wake someone up."

"Yeah," Stumps agreed. "We need a rope."

"Laure will come look for us eventually . . . ?" I was holding someone's sleeping bag. I could have thrown it but I was cold. I sank down with it against the wall.

"I'm gonna see if I can find another way out," Stumps said. "You guys?"

I couldn't move. I couldn't talk.

Mitch glanced at me. "We'll wait with the stuff here. Till help comes."

"Gotcha. Catch y'alls." Stumps snapped his tattooed fingers and then paused and stepped back to Mitch. "You're a champ, my man." He engulfed Mitch, who was so much broader and bulkier, in a shoulder-slapping hug. Then Stumps gave me a wink and salute and disappeared down the hole in the roof.

I untied the sleeping bag and wrapped it around my shoulders and Mitch eased himself down against the wall near me. From the stiffness of his movements, I could see he was as worn out as I was. He'd done a lot. He didn't even know these people.

"Want to share this?" I asked, holding up the sleeping bag.

He scooted in and took the edge of the bag. He couldn't pull it around his shoulder without getting closer. His trying not to touch me made it suddenly awkward for us to be alone.

To break the silence I asked, "So, you have a history of breaking-and-entering?"

"Stealing, breaking-and-entering, you name it." His voice was husky and low. "My dad thought I belonged in juvie. He threw me out of the house."

"Did he come around?" I yawned.

"No, he died."

"Oh, crap. I'm sorry." I wrapped my arms around my knees. "What about your mom?"

"Still in Boston," Mitch said. "She's relieved to have me out of her hair, I can tell you that."

"I know what that's like." Some people were so sentimental about moms, like they're all unconditional love and hot apple pie. I knew better.

"Yeah? Well, maybe that's why you're . . . You know, you said I was treating you like a girl; the thing is, you're not like . . . I just never knew a girl who was . . . You're really tough."

I smiled wryly, wondering if I should take that as a compliment.

"You cold?" he asked, his voice close to my ear.

"Yeah."

"Come here." He reached his arm around my shoulder, his whole body suddenly against mine, his breath on my face and stubbled cheek on my skin.

I jumped, scrambling to my feet. I put my hands over my face, embarrassed and confused. "What . . . why are you even here?"

He tucked his chin, hiding his face behind his hood. "I know what *you're* doing here," he said sullenly. "You worship these losers."

"No, I—" The building shook, knocking me off balance, and I grabbed the wall of Laure's building.

Mitch jumped to his feet. "The crane!" he exclaimed, pointing.

It was the wrecking crane swinging into action. The sun was up, somehow it had become morning. The crane smashed into the top floor of Rot-Squat. Bricks crumbled in an avalanche to the street, and just like that, the attic room that used to be Lee's, where I had patched Raven's jeans in the summer, where we had just been an hour ago, had a gaping hole in it with the room's unpainted sheetrock, dirty sheets, books, and CDs exposed to the frosty winter air.

"I can help you up—you can find a rope or a ladder or something!" Mitch yelled. "You can get help!" He held his hands in a stirrup.

I looked desperately up the steep wall of the building. I put my hand on his shoulder for balance but another hit of the crane made me stumble. I tried again and Mitch hoisted me up with a grunt. "Onto my shoulders!" he said, and I scrambled, leaving filthy boot prints all over his coat.

From his shoulders, I could get my arms over the ledge but I wasn't strong enough to pull myself up. I tried to get a foothold on the wall and a face appeared over the ledge. The neighbor with the long dreadlocks. Like Rapunzel, I thought wildly, throw down your dreads. Hands grabbed my elbows, helping me up.

"Well, good morning to you!" the man said. There were more neighbors on the roof, in slippers and coats thrown over pajamas; they'd been woken by the shakes of the wrecking crane, and came up to the roof to see what was happening. They were looking at the piles of backpacks and bags and at me.

"Mitch!" I pointed over the wall. The crane hit again, shaking us even here, two buildings away, like an earthquake.

"I've got a fire ladder downstairs!" a guy announced, and hurried off.

"Hold on!" Laure cried over the ledge to Mitch.

When he crested the parapet, helped by two neighbors and the fire ladder, it was a huge relief, though the roar of crowd noise rising from the street below was a surprise. There were people down there now? Had they seen him?

Someone pointed, open mouthed, at the roof of Rot-

Squat. There was a figure there, on the edge of the broken, jagged roof. A man, silhouetted against the sky.

"Oh my god, it's Stumps," I breathed.

He gave a yodeling mountaintop cry, five stories above the street, and waved his arms.

The crane lurched over the street. It couldn't continue now, they'd kill him! It stalled with a frustrated stutter. We all gaped—Mitch, me, the neighbors around us, people on roofs and in windows all along the block. People cheered and screamed. Stumps, on the edge of the destroyed roof, dropped his pants and mooned the officers below.

Mitch and I rested while Laure and her sister and their neighbors got the remainder of the rescued belongings from the roof next door down to the apartment. I couldn't keep my eyes open. I drifted off in the bedroom, then woke when the building started rumbling again from the crane. I stumbled out to the living room, where Laure's sister was standing at her window with a mug of coffee. The backpacks and bundles took up most of her floor, but the pile looked pathetically small, really, when you considered how hard we'd worked and how much had been lost.

"Where's Mitch?" I asked. He wasn't lying on her velvet couch where I'd last seen him.

"He said he had to go to work," she said sympathetically. "Poor guy. Laure told the dungeon you're not coming in today. Let me get you some coffee."

"What time is it?" I asked. The building rumbled with another shake.

"Close to noon." She gestured at the noise. "They just got that boy off the roof, finally. He was on the morning news! He kept dancing out of their way. The cops were so scared up there on the roof, they couldn't get him! It was quite the little drama!"

"I have to go." I couldn't believe I'd slept and missed all that. I ran down the stairs and peeked out the front door. The block was dusty with debris falling from Rot-Squat. An officer in a hard hat escorted me fast to the intersection and past the barricades. I found Raven there in the crowd. She looked like she had slept less than I had. When I told her how much stuff we had stashed at Laure's, her eyes filled up and she hugged me and we swayed together to the earthquake rumble of destruction.

While the police had been dealing with Stumps, she said, she and a bunch of her housemates had gone downtown with a lawyer. A judge had issued a stay of demolition, saying the squatters must be allowed to get their belongings out before the building was leveled. But Giuliani wasn't taking any chances. He'd ignored the judge's order and started the demolition again as soon as Stumps was off the roof. A dust cloud consumed Avenue B around the crumbling corpse of Rot-Squat, shock by shock. The lawyer was on the block shaking her paperwork at the OEM men who wouldn't listen.

I sat on a stoop, in a crowd of other cold and miserable people, waiting for it to be over. Should I go home? I wasn't doing anything useful, but it felt wrong to leave.

I watched a hooded figure come down the street, tall and substantial in Carhartt and red-and-white sneakers. He looked so reassuringly familiar I found myself— before my tired brain even put together who it was— floating toward him.

"You went to work," I cried, as if I'd been abandoned.

"Boss said I was a zombie, sent me home." Mitch's eyes flicked over my face. He reached for the arm I held out. "I figured you'd still be here." He said it flatly, but the meaning moved through my frozen limbs with warm certainty. He'd come to get me.

X

Veronica and I took her boss's van to Laure's sister's place the next Sunday. The bundles and backpacks filled up the back of the van; it looked like a lot, and we drove down to 5th Street Squat feeling triumphant.

Earplugs was out front waiting and he joined us at the rear of the vehicle. He whistled when Veronica opened the back doors. "This is some badass shit you pulled," he said.

A bunch of Rot-Squatters showed up together.

Abby jumped on me, her long skinny arms tight around me. "Holy shit! Look at all this!"

"You are such a hero!" Raven's eyes were wide and she clutched her heart. "You totally rock, Sid!"

Everyone started pulling stuff out onto the sidewalk. Eli and Lydia introduced themselves to me. I felt like Santa Claus, digging their bag out of the van. They'd just had the worst week of their lives but I felt secretly elated. All these people knew who I was, Veronica looked at me with respect, they called me a hero and it felt true.

"I've been recovering all week," I told everyone. "I bruised my tailbone falling when we snuck in there, and then my arms were so worn out from throwing stuff, I

could barely lift them over my head to put a shirt on!"
They all laughed.

A kid I didn't know with stringy hair and a cap said,
"Stumps told me you got some of my tools?" It was the
carpenter with the neat room. I dug under the van seat
for the Makita box.

"We put a couple chisels in there," I showed him.

Lee had come out of 5th Street, imposing and tall
with a knit hat pulled over his dreads. "Let's get it all
inside," he directed the guys with him.

"Actually, we can bring some of it to C-Squat," Raven said. "Like Meg's stuff and Gibby's and—"

"Let's just get it inside," Lee cut her off. "Sort it out
there. Unless you girls like crying out here on the street
better."

"*Hello*," Abby scowled at him, "this is, like, the first
happy thing since the eviction!"

"There's no happy thing," Lee replied with disgust.
He turned to the stringy-haired kid holding the Makita
drill. "You happy, Davey? You feel like celebrating with
the rest of your tools in a fuckin' landfill in Staten Island?"

Lee grabbed some more stuff off the sidewalk and
went in the house and the guys followed him. The kid
with the drill looked deflated and I remembered his tidy
workbench and I didn't feel so great anymore. When we
were done, I got back in the van with Veronica. We drove
up Avenue B and passed where Rot-Squat had been. It
hit me in the gut now: the empty space. Everything, the
building and the lives inside it. Carted away by dump

truck. Now there was a chain-link fence around a little square of rubble. It looked so small, you couldn't believe a whole building had stood there. Someone had put a votive candle and flowers in front of the fence and then it had snowed and now it was just a dingy wet lump.

I saved newspapers following the eviction but I'd barely looked at them. After my day playing Santa Claus, I felt depressed and didn't want to think about any of it. But a couple weeks later on a Saturday morning, I started looking through it all. It was quiet in the house. Lorenzo, Skip, and Eddie all hung out by Lorenzo's stove now and I hardly saw any of them. I heard their voices behind the curtains when I went in and out the front door and I felt left out. Lorenzo had been civil enough to tell me about the eviction, but I still didn't know where we stood, if we were friends again. I was too wary to risk making a move. He could still make a thing about how I'd hit him if he wanted to. I cut out the articles to paste in my sketchbook. There was Stumps dancing on the roof in the Metro section of the *Times*. The *Daily News* called him a madman. The *Post* made it sound like the place had burned down. The only article that mentioned the stay of demolition that Giuliani had ignored was in the *Voice*.

The picture of Stumps made me think about Mitch and where we'd been when Stumps was up on the roof. I hadn't seen much of Mitch since then; he was working a lot. I never would have thought he'd do so much to help the squatters he usually dismissed as dust-smoking scammers. But he loved buildings and he hated being told where he could and couldn't go. A *No Trespassing* sign was like a dare to him. When he talked about getting around those kinds of rules, his voice got happy and quick, like when he told me about the cabin in Maine where he was going to live someday.

The day he'd come to get me on Avenue B, we'd talked the whole way home about squatting, and I kept thinking about everything he'd said. He told me he'd learned from an old New York squatter he met in Boston how to go downtown and pull records on who owned a building. When you had a lead on a good place, he said, maybe you snuck in a back window to make sure no one was using it. But when you left, you went out the front door and installed your own lock. Neighbors who saw someone sneaking in a window would call the cops, but a clean-cut guy going in the front door with a key? No problem. "You just wanna look nondescript and confident," he explained. "Then you count on how self-absorbed city people are. And you're invisible."

For Mitch, squatting was all about buildings. He said, "Those punk kids make no sense to me. If they really had to squat a building, they wouldn't look so crazy. Do they want to go out to Brooklyn and really fix a place up? No, they'd rather live all piled up on each other like rats. They're *scenesters*, not squatters."

"You make it sound easy to be a scenester!" I had replied. "I wanted more than anything to be let into one of these overcrowded places. I would never have gone out to Brooklyn if I had a choice." I didn't want to sound ungrateful so I added, "But I'm glad I did." It was true. I'd gotten used to Brooklyn. I felt tough living out there. And after what had happened to Rot-Squat and how the Lower East Side was changing, remote, unlovely Brooklyn seemed like a smarter place to be.

"Knock, knock," Skip's voice startled me back to the present, and I looked up. He was in my doorway holding a jacket I'd promised to mend.

"Come in." I dug around in my trunk for brown thread.

"Lorenzo told us about what you and Mitch did there." He pointed at the newspaper clippings.

I smiled at my fingers threading the needle. "Skip, how did you meet Mitch and move in here?"

"Did I never tell you about that?" He perched on the edge of my easy chair. "Me and Eddie were looking for a building out here. The place up in Harlem got so bad. Drugs and stuff. We crashed a couple nights at a place around the corner and then we met Mitch at the hardware store. I don't know how he knew we were squatters."

"He really reads people, doesn't he?" I mused. "Then what?"

"This place was in much better shape. Mitch had done a lot already. And he needed help, you know, people to help secure it and be around and stuff."

He watched my fingers on his coat, the needle gliding in and out where the seam was split up the side.

"You know, Mitch acts all in charge," he went on, "but we're all necessary here. We should all have equal say. If you and Mitch are on good terms, maybe you can talk to him about us having a house meeting?" Skip was like a broken record. The more he harped on about house meetings, the more stubbornly Mitch scoffed.

Lights made me glance out the window. There was a fire truck pulled up, and firemen climbing out. We heard a knock on the door below "Shit! What do they want?" We looked at each other in alarm, then we ran for Mitch's room in back.

"The door!" Skip and I cried at the same time. "Firemen!"

Mitch threw the book he was reading aside and pulled on sneakers. "Is there a fire?"

"I don't know! I don't smell anything." I raced to the window on the side and looked out, but I couldn't see anything. There was pounding on the front door. Skip and I followed Mitch down the stairs.

"What are we going to do?" I called to Mitch's back.

Eddie was in the doorway of his bedroom on the second floor, hands in the pockets of a giant green hoodie. He joined the stampede down the stairs and we all arrived in a row in the foyer. Lorenzo was already there. He had a ski mask pulled over his face and was dragging a metal pipe to the door.

"Help me with this," he barked at Mitch.

"What the hell are you doing?" Mitch boomed.

"Barricading!" Lorenzo spat. "The fuck you think?"

The door shook again. "Open up. Fire Department."

"What can we do for you, sir?" Mitch called back.

"You've got a woodstove. We just need to take a look. Routine inspection."

"Get that out of here. We're letting them in," Mitch hissed at Lorenzo. He grabbed the other end of the pipe and the two of them faced each other like a game of tug-of-war.

Lorenzo turned to me, his eyes dark holes in the mask. "Sid!" he rasped. "What you think?"

"Me?" I looked behind me, like I would find another Sid there, but it was just Eddie and Skip, both looking at me with round nervous eyes.

"Yeah, *you!*" Lorenzo spat. "After Rot-Squat, you wanna let these bastards in?"

"I . . . Don't they just . . ." I stammered. Why was everyone staring at me?

The fist pounded the door again. "Come on now, you don't want to make us enter the hard way."

With a shove of the pipe, Mitch knocked Lorenzo off balance, then unbolted the door.

There were three of them, a wall of rubber coats, boots, and giant hats. The guy in front looked Mitch up and down. "You in charge here, son?"

"Yes sir," Mitch answered.

Lorenzo cursed under his breath, and stomped into his room.

Mitch ushered the firemen up the stairs. Skip and I scurried behind, and waited on the second floor by my unfinished mural. We could hear Mitch upstairs show-ing the men around. He was prepared for this, there was a note in his voice that sounded like pride. He had a fire extinguisher, test sticker up to date. Sand buckets. Kin-dling and paper stored at the correct distance. But what would Lorenzo's stove downstairs look like?

Eddie joined me and Skip. He leaned against the wall and started rolling a cigarette. "So, Sid," he started, conversationally, "it true you doin' phone sex now?"

Did he think we were hanging out here for fun? Like a party? "No!" I stared at him. "Who said that? I just answer the phone at a place." I peered up the stairs; the firemen were coming back down.

"Well, you got a real nice voice, Sid, I bet you're good at that." He nodded with a vacant half-smile at the bulky firemen, clanking past us like storm troopers. We all followed them down the stairs. Mitch waved good-bye with a military salute and bolted the door behind them, then looked up at me and grinned in relief.

"Phew!" I smiled back. They hadn't suspected there was a second stove; both were tied into the same chim-ney. The way Mitch had shoved Lorenzo was a little shocking, but Mitch had made it okay with the fire-men and hid the second stove, so it was forgivable, I thought—until I saw Lorenzo's face.

He was red and scowling in the doorway with his fists clenched and the muscles in his neck taut with an-ger, but when he spoke, his voice was slow and steady: "You think you in *charge* here?"

Everyone turned to look at him; his controlled rage was frightening.

"You want to get us all kicked out?" Mitch responded. He was sweating from running up and down the stairs and breathing hard. "What does your stove even look like in there? You probably have shit everywhere! I covered for you!"

"This dude say he in charge," Lorenzo turned to Skip. "This okay with you?"

Mitch spun around, looking at us all. I didn't catch his eye.

Skip mumbled, "Oh, someone cares what I think?"

The silence in the cramped foyer was deafening. Lorenzo looked smug. He knew he wasn't the only one with a grudge.

Now Mitch was really on the defensive. "Oh, come on. We had to . . ." He raised his arms to gesture and in the small space, Skip flinched back.

Eddie stepped forward quickly like he needed to defend Skip. "Hey now." He crossed his barbell-thick arms like a bodyguard. "Let's not get excited."

Mitch stared at Eddie, taken aback. Behind him, Skip muttered, "You *told* them you were in *charge*."

Lorenzo saw his dog pack circling. There was a smile in his voice, as well as a snarl, when he said, "Who fuckin' elected *you*?"

While I watched, Lorenzo and Eddie and Skip grew taller and Mitch shrank.

"You know what?" Mitch finally said. "You losers

want to ruin this place? Suit yourselves. You can all go to hell." He stomped up the stairs.

"Bye bye, now!" Lorenzo called after him.

"Can you believe that jerk?" Skip's voice was excited. He followed Lorenzo into his room. "What a brownnoser."

I heard Lorenzo say, "Let's have that whiskey, man, I need a fuckin' drink."

Eddie gave me a wink and patted my arm as he passed me to join them. I heard chairs scrape around Lorenzo's stove as they settled in.

I stood in Mitch's doorway upstairs. Arched windows on the west side of his room overlooked the BQE and a domed skylight splashed waning afternoon light on the brick walls. Mitch was pulling clothes off a rack.

"What do you want?"

"Are you leaving?"

"I'm not cut out for this *commune* shit," he spat. "If you all want to throw our house in the toilet . . . I give up."

I didn't like being lumped in with "everyone" and yelled at. I couldn't talk to Mitch when he was like this; it was pointless. I turned away.

To my surprise, he followed and grabbed my arm. "You know what would have happened if we did it Lorenzo's way, don't you?" He towered over me, big and angry.

"What?"

"If you don't let the fire department in," he spoke through clenched teeth, landing hard on each word, "they can say you're a hazard and in twenty-four hours you're out on your ass. They're the only city agency that has that power."

"I don't . . . I didn't know . . ."

"Yeah, maybe you don't know that. Maybe Lorenzo doesn't either." He leaned closer, his face ugly and red. "Or maybe he's thinking getting evicted doesn't look so bad."

"That's crazy!" I shook my arm free of his grip.

"Look at those Rot-Squat punks," Mitch hissed. "They're heroes now. Working-class fucking heroes. Lorenzo would be one of them, and he'd be taken in on the Lower East Side, where he is all the time anyways. Nice story, right? He tried to fight the fire department off single-handed, right? You think he wants to be out here in Brooklyn? You think he gives a shit about the rest of us? No way. This rock-star punk thing . . . bullshit. Lorenzo is out for number one."

I stared at Mitch, shocked by his venom.

His lip curled. "I guess I thought you were better than that." He turned and walked into his bedroom, and shut the door.

What the hell did that even mean? I was supposed to go meet Raven anyway, and at this point I just wanted to get away from the house and everyone in it. I grabbed my messenger bag out of my room and rushed out. Maybe Mitch was somewhat right about Lorenzo, but he took it too far. No one wanted to get evicted. I marched to the subway, fuming. I hated how Mitch had yelled at me and I hadn't had the gumption to say anything back. I'd been too shocked, too hurt. Well, if he suspected me of sympathizing with Lorenzo, he was goddamn right. I thought of Lee and what he might say. We'd seen at Rot-Squat how quickly the authorities fucked us over when they got the chance, so why should we play fair? Being a squatter meant you got to say fuck you to all the people who thought they were in charge with their stupid rules.

"He's jealous," Raven said, when I told her everything. She looked like an East Village hipster in her new polyester jeans. The neighborhood had put together a clothes drive for the Rot-Squatters who had lost everything. She said all she needed to buy were socks and underwear so we headed down Broadway to Canal Jeans.

"Mitch? Jealous? Of what?"

"Of Lorenzo and you! He was the dude with you at the eviction, right? Totally likes you. He's cute."

"Cute?"

"Big hands . . ." She nudged me playfully. "You know what they say!" The whole day Mitch had spent outside Rot-Squat no one had talked to him, but Raven had noticed his hands?

"Well, whatever. You can't sleep with your housemates!"

"Ha! You tell me now?" Raven laughed.

"But . . . it's like sleeping with someone you work with!"

"Which is the *best*! It makes work so much less boring!"

She told me about some girl at the coffee shop who was vibing her. But maybe she wouldn't have to work at all if Rot-Squat won their court case. The lawyer said they had a good case because of the stay of demolition Giuliani had ignored. The lawyer said they'd start by asking for a hundred thousand dollars each to replace their lost belongings. Raven walked faster as she talked. She could buy land in Belize with that money. Stumps was going to buy a building in Brooklyn. Meg and some others were going to open a vegan restaurant.

"That's why Lee is being such a dick," she said. "He lived at Rot-Squat so long and then moved out just in time to not get anything. Bad karma, it's totally what he deserves."

"Why'd he leave Rot-Squat anyways?"

"He got in this, like, feud with Blue and Gibby and those guys. I guess it started about drugs in the house 'cause Lee wanted to make all these rules, like pot's okay but no white drugs, no pills, and it's kind of bullshit 'cause he takes pills all the time. And he's all like, attacking everyone—*seriously*! They ended up in this thing with a baseball bat, he fractured Gibby's arm, but then he and Jess broke up and he left. But now he's all like, if there's money coming down he was in the house before everyone, which is basically true but it's not, like, *relevant* 'cause the lawyer says our only chance is to get money for lost *possessions* not for the house or work we put in or anything, because the case for adverse possession got thrown out, the judge won't even hear that. And Lee wasn't living there when it happened. Which he should be grateful for, really. Right?"

I hurried to keep up. My mind kept skipping back to what she had said about Mitch. Could she be right? Could he really like me? What had she seen that made her think so? There was that moment on the roof . . . It dawned on me that if he was into me, all that stuff he'd been saying earlier would make more sense. He'd been afraid that I'd sided against him. His anger was scary, but maybe underneath it, he was just hurt.

Mitch wasn't at home when I got back. I figured he'd stay somewhere else to cool off. I could talk to him when he returned, even if he just dropped by to get his stuff.

I hung around the house as much as possible the next couple days, afraid I'd miss him. And then on Friday night I got home from work and there he was. Sitting at the kitchen table reading a magazine. I stood at the top of the third-floor stairs with my stomach suddenly all butterflies, trying to remember what I wanted to say or how we talked to each other.

Then he turned his head and it wasn't Mitch at all. It was a boy with floppy green hair.

"Jimmy! Where's Mitch?"

"Gone, dude!" Jimmy leaned back in the chair and put his long legs on the kitchen table. He held up the bagel he was eating. "I dumpstered a bag of these, want one?"

"Where'd he go?"

He cocked his head at me and his bangs fell out of his eyes. "Who?"

"Mitch!"

Jimmy shrugged. "He just called and said I could have his room if I wanted." I guess living with the girl-friend didn't work out. Anyways, the worst of winter was over, it wasn't so bad now.

"But . . . his stuff . . ." I stepped to the bedroom door and peered in. It looked totally different than it had on Sunday. Clean and empty. Jimmy's duffel bag slumped next to the stripped mattress.

"He left this," Jimmy said. Mitch's boom box was gone from the windowsill and my Green Day CD that Mitch loved was lying caseless on the kitchen table. "That's so Mitch to buy the major label sellout shit. Probably never heard of Lookout, right?"

"Yeah," I said. "I'll get rid of it."

There was a pit in my stomach. I went into my bed-room and threw the CD against the wall. No goodbye, no note? After Rot-Squat and everything? The CD fell onto the floor and I kicked it under my chair into a pile of jeans and dirty socks. I was furious with Mitch for making me feel abandoned. And I was furious with my-self for letting it get to me.

"Whatever," I said aloud, flopping onto my bed. "Who needs you and your stupid soup anyways? I hope you go to Maine and get eaten by a moose."

XI

I hadn't meant to tell anyone at work that I was a squatter. People had weird ideas about it, like that it meant you slept in a cardboard box like a homeless person, or in some derelict building you snuck into through a hole in a fence. But after running into Laure at the eviction of Rot-Squat, the cat was out of the bag and they wanted to hear all about it. Kathy said I was a genius, living in the city rent-free. Laure had a million bird-brained questions about how it worked. She wanted to know how we could control who was in our squat if we didn't have legal permission to be there ourselves. If she showed up with her suitcase one day and wanted to move in, what right would I have to keep her out? That was how she imagined one got a room in a squat, just by being ballsy.

I explained that once we'd established ourselves in a building we had legal and ethical human rights like any other tenant. We had a lock on the door and we decided who got a key and who to let in. It sounded good when I said it. But in that free-falling moment before sleep, when the confidence of the day dissolved, Laure's version of things seemed as plausible as mine. I'd always thought of the Bakery as Mitch's house, where the rest of us just lived. Mitch had taken responsibility for every aspect of the building including who moved in. He had approved each of us with his gut instincts. Without him, there was something random about the collection of us at the house now. I pictured us each as little cogs in a machine someone had taken apart. Only Mitch knew how and why we all fit together.

But I guess I was the only one who felt that way. After Mitch left, Skip called a house meeting and everyone came. It was starting to feel like spring, the days were longer, everyone was ready to come out of their shells. At the meeting Lorenzo and Jimmy were chiming in with ideas for house projects. We spent a day cleaning out the foyer and replacing the broken fixture so we could have a light in there. I mentioned that Mitch had told me it shorted out because it was wired wrong and everyone looked blank, like, *Mitch who?* We cleaned some graffiti off the front of the building and I painted the door bright green while Skip and Jimmy picked up the trash on the sidewalk in front of the house. Lorenzo got out his broom and pretended he was the maid, mincing around like he was in high heels and everyone laughed. I looked around and saw how relaxed everyone was, having fun and working together. The building looked so good cleaned up. Mitch had taken all the tension and anger with him. It was better now; it was spring.

Jimmy got a job barbacking at Sweetwater, the neighborhood punk hangout. I went to visit him on a Friday night at the end of June. I was settling on a stool near Jimmy's perch at the bar when a pretty girl with a cloud of pale hair and violet lips burst out of the back room and almost clobbered me with a pool cue.

"Abby!" I hugged her back. "Nice dress!" Gone was the shapeless Carhartt coverall she'd worn at the eviction of Rot-Squat. Now she was a Courtney Love baby doll in pink and artfully shredded tights.

"I'm working at a vintage store on St. Mark's," she explained. "But I'm staying out here in Brooklyn! I knew I'd run into you! I can't believe this guy is back here too."

She gestured at Jimmy, who leaned on the bar with his faded Mohawk shoved into a baseball cap and his Suicidal Tendencies T-shirt tight around his narrow chest. He grinned at Abby, eyeing her hungrily. "Back in Black!" he sang.

"Your turn, babe." A man appeared behind Abby, wrapping tattooed fingers around her gauzy waist, his wide, scarred face looming over her shoulder.

"Babe, this is Sid," Abby introduced us. "From the Brooklyn squat I told you about! Sid, this is Nick."

She flitted back to the pool table while we shook hands. He pointed to his buddies, big thuggy-looking guys around the pool table, and told me they used to squat too, back in the day.

Jimmy jumped in: "Then y'all gotta come see our place! Come hang out!"

Nick leaned back on his heels, planted his pool cue

on the tile floor, and studied Jimmy. Finally he said, "I'd like that."

"I'd like it too!" Jimmy nodded and grinned like an idiot. "I'd like that a lot!"

Nick left to take his turn and Jimmy whispered to me, "What the hell was that?"

"He was deciding whether or not you're a fag."

"Look at them. Beauty and the beast, right?"

I followed his gaze to the back room. Abby leaned over Nick, who was setting up a shot at the pool table, and planted a purple kiss on his cheek. His friends laughed. The goofy, smitten smile made his pockmarked face look sweet.

"Abby's living with him?" I asked Jimmy.

"She only moved in with him because she had nowhere to go," Jimmy answered peevishly. "But I hear he's bad news. He used to drum in Knuckle Head and they kicked him out 'cause he's violent."

"Dude, you cannot be jealous," I said. "You had your chance." When he'd been seeing Abby back at Rot-Squat, he'd played the field until she got fed up. She'd hooked up with him again that time at our house after Lorenzo's show, but Jimmy hadn't been bothered to keep it going then. He didn't care at all until she sashayed into Sweetwater with a boyfriend looking all happy. Guys only want what they can't have.

"How can she sleep with that gorilla?" Jimmy frowned. "He's wearing white socks."

The bartender asked Jimmy to grab a case from storage and I followed him into the back room. Abby put me on a doubles team with a friend who was part of their crew, a woman around thirty, like the rest of Nick's friends. She drummed in an all-girl punk band, and she loved that I squatted out here with a bunch of guys—she was my instant best friend. The big thuggy dudes wanted to hear all about the place too. They pounded Jimmy on the shoulder when he passed with the crate of beer. "We're coming to see the place!" one of them growled, showing his missing tooth.

No one tried to get in on the pool table while Nick and his friends were dominating it, so we were on our third or fourth game when Abby pointed to the crowded bar and said, "Hey, it's Lorenzo!"

Lorenzo was flushed like he'd just ridden his bike over the bridge; probably from band practice. I watched Jimmy emerge from behind the bar and fist bump him. Lorenzo squeezed in by the bar to get a beer and Jimmy shoved his way through the crowd toward us with a plastic tub held over his head. "Sid, your boy's here!" Jimmy called out as he headed to the ice machine.

"Who's your boy?" the drummer girl asked, her lips around the straw in her vodka drink.

"He just means our housemate." I glared at Jimmy's back.

"Jimmy told me about your fight!" Abby leaned in all bright-eyed. She loved trouble and she was tipsy. "You totally punched him, right?"

"Who'd Sid punch?" Nick wrapped his arm around Abby.

"That Mexican kid with the dreads," Abby pointed. "What'd he do, anyways?"

I finished my beer. "He pissed me off."

Nick guffawed and slapped my shoulder. "That's right. Sid here's a brawler," he announced to his friends. "My Abby's a brawler too, right? What's that story you told me, babe? Fighting the girl on Avenue B, didn't you rip her top off?"

Jimmy was pushing past us on his way back to the bar with his tub full of ice. He'd heard Nick and he flinched, nervous. Jimmy had been there on Avenue B; the fight was over him. If Nick knew that, he probably wouldn't think the story was funny. Abby squirmed out of Nick's grasp. "Babe, give me a quarter," she said, and pranced off to the jukebox.

One of Nick's friends called after her, "You play the Pixies again, I'm gonna put this pool cue through my eye."

Lorenzo came toward us with a beer. Everyone watched him curiously but he didn't even glance at me. He went straight to Abby at the jukebox. She smiled and put up her hand to give a little wave, but he leaned in and kissed each of her pretty, pale cheeks, one after the other, European style.

When the bar closed, Jimmy led the whole stumbling gang back to the Bakery. Abby linked her arm in mine and we walked together and tried to ignore Nick and his friends, who were behind us making fun of Lorenzo. His bike, his accent, his hair. The familiar way Lorenzo had greeted Abby had rubbed Nick the wrong way. Luckily, Nick and his friends were so incoherent and drunk that it was plausible Lorenzo wasn't registering any of it. I asked Abby if she'd seen Raven lately.

"No," she said. "God, she's so caught up in the court case, it's all she does and, like, she makes me feel guilty that I'm not sending press releases out every time the judge farts or whatever, but it just seems pointless, you know?"

"I guess she just wants to keep busy."

"I don't think we'll really get any money," Abby said. "All the kids from the other houses hate us now. Everyone felt sorry at first and wanted to help, before they thought we were going to be rich. I'm over it. I'm just saving up to go to California." She slapped a hand over her mouth and snuck a look behind her at Nick and his friends. "Don't say anything about that, 'kay?" she giggled. Clearly Nick wasn't part of her long-term plans.

Jimmy ushered us all in the house. The tension was palpable and it pushed his host act into hysteria. He tap-danced across the pitch-black third floor into his room, pointing out obstacles, flipping lights, pulling kitchen chairs into his room. He put on a Dead Kennedys tape, found a beer opener, and mugged like a clown getting everyone settled.

"This is awesome," Abby's drummer friend exclaimed. She sat on Jimmy's bed next to Abby. The house did seem nice in the summer, with all the big windows open and a breeze wafting through. "You guys were so smart to squat this place, it's huge!"

It was weird being in Mitch's room without him; that must have been why I said out loud what I'd been thinking: "We didn't squat it, we just live here."

"Whas'at suppose to mean?" Lorenzo snapped, like I'd called him a poseur. He sat all tense on the edge of a kitchen chair, staring daggers around the room.

"I mean Mitch broke in here when it was an empty building. *He* squatted it. The rest of us just moved in."

"Who's Mitch?" Nick asked.

"Oh, Mitch!" Abby cried. "He's the one who got our stuff out of Rot-Squat with you, right?"

"Big fuckin' hero," Lorenzo muttered.

"You're sitting in his room."

"I'm sittin' in *my own* fuckin' house," snapped Lorenzo. "Drinkin' a beer. Y'got a problem?"

"*You lookin' at me?*" Nick mocked. His friends snorted like horses ready for action.

I looked down and picked at my beer label. I didn't mean to cause trouble for Lorenzo, but I didn't want to let it go. "Just show some respect," I mumbled.

"For your *boyfriend*."

"Shut up!"

"Hey, you heard the lady," Nick chimed in.

"Whatever, you love that dude," Lorenzo said, then raised his voice high, "*Mitch say this, Mitch say that, Mitch blah blah blah* . . ." He bobbled his head in a girly way.

Jimmy laughed, spitting beer out of his mouth. "Ha! Okay, Sid, he's got you there."

"Really?" I was surprised. Did I really talk about Mitch that much? And if I did, why would Lorenzo care?

"Where's the facilities?" Abby stood, stretching her long arms over her head, which raised her tiny dress almost to her crotch. Nick slapped her ass and she winced.

Jimmy jumped up. "I'll show you. Who needs a beer?"

"Right here," Nick said.

Jimmy and Abby left the room and the drummer girl leaned toward me. "So you were the one who broke into Rot-Squat? We heard about that!"

I started telling them about the coincidence of the girl who I worked with living next door, and how she got Mitch and me past the police barricade, but I was aware of Nick fidgeting and scowling at the door.

"What happened to that beer?" Nick finally interrupted. He lurched to his feet and staggered out of Jimmy's lamp-lit room into the darkness. Then the silence was pierced by a shriek and we all jumped. There was a sickening thud of flesh and a crash and Jimmy yelped like a puppy.

We ran into the dark kitchen. I tripped over a chair, fumbling for the light on the table. Jimmy was sprawled on the ground, holding his face, Abby was screaming, and Nick's steel-toed shoe was raised, aimed at Jimmy's ribs.

"Stop him!" The drummer girl threw herself at Nick, and Nick's big friends, who had looked like they wouldn't mind getting a kick or two in themselves, stumbled into action, pulling Nick away.

"You little shit, I'm gonna kill you!" Nick yelled.

"Get him out of here!" Abby screamed.

"Abby, get away from him!" Nick cried from the stairs. "We're leaving!"

Abby stood up, her boots planted. "You're crazy!" Her lipstick was a violet smear. "I'm not going anywhere with you!"

The men quickly disappeared downstairs, I could hear them arguing and pushing Nick across the second floor beneath us. Jimmy was still on the floor and I was frozen with my hand on the kitchen lamp. How bad was Jimmy hurt? Would we need to get him to a hospital? I took a step toward him and then he groaned, "Abby!" and she threw herself down next to him. Jimmy's arm snaked up into her hair and pulled her close.

I heard a chuckle behind me. Lorenzo was leaning against the doorframe, his arms crossed. "Don't worry," he rolled his eyes, "he's fine."

Noon the next day, Nick was back. He pounded the front door with a baseball bat. "*Whore!*" floated in with the sound of light Sunday traffic and birds. My room was at the front of the building so it was as clear as if he was standing next to me. But all the windows in the house were open, like everyone else's on the street, so

I wasn't the only one who could hear. I pulled on my boots, walked across the kitchen, and paused at Jimmy's door, wishing I didn't have to intrude. Then I heard pounding again, and "*Cunt!*" and I knocked.

"What?" Jimmy called, and I pushed the door open. "He's back."

Abby sat up and pulled her dress over her head. Jimmy put a hand on his swollen face and groaned. The bag of frozen peas—which I'd walked six blocks last night to get for his black eye, since Abby and he were too scared to leave—lay in a puddle on the floor.

Footsteps on the stairs made me spin around. Skip, Eddie, Lorenzo.

"That man's going to break the door," Skip said. His eyes widened as Abby climbed out of Jimmy's bed in her pink dress, her legs bare and her hair a wild blond halo under the skylight. "What's *she* doing here?"

"Should we call the cops?" I bit a fingernail.

Jimmy snorted. "How?" The pay phone was a block away. "I'm not going out there."

"Nick's terrified of cops," Abby said. "He has warrants."

"*Bitch!*" came up from below, with a new flurry of pounding.

Skip pointed at Abby again. "This is *her* problem, not ours! She's got to go!"

"She can't go out there! She'll get hurt!"

"We can't call the cops!" Skip insisted, fists clenched by his sides. "They can't come here. What if he breaks the door? What if the cops want to bust in? This looks *so* bad."

"Sid," Eddie turned to me, like I was the one being unreasonable, "the lady's gotta go to her man, smooth things over."

"Absolutely not! He's dangerous."

"We could lose our *house!*" Skip protested.

The pounding resonated through the building. "*Whore!*"

Skip put his hands in his hair. "This is what I mean! Couples mess up *everything!* This has to *stop!*"

"Sid should go," Lorenzo spoke up for the first time. "Me? What?"

"Go out and tell him to chill. He's not gonna hit *you*. Go, hurry up."

Everyone looked at me. What could I do? I threw up my hands in defeat and marched down the stairs with no idea what I would say when I got there. I opened the door and surprised Nick midswing and he stumbled. I pulled the freshly painted door shut behind me and right away I heard the bolt slip back into place. Great. Skip had followed me down and locked me out.

"She with that little punk?" Nick jabbed a finger near my face.

"You have to stop!" Across the street I saw a face in a window; a woman with a baby. The whole block was probably watching. I hissed, "Abby's staying with me 'cause you scared her last night. Nothing's going on, calm down."

"I *saw* them!" he yelled. "I want that punk down here. Now."

"What's that going to do?" Over Nick's shoulder I watched a cop car glide silently up to the curb. A neighbor must have called. Nick didn't hear anything until the door opened, then he spun around and dropped his bat with a startled look. Before he could take a step, a petite lady cop was out of the car and on him like a ninja. I didn't even see what happened, I just heard him grunt and she had him pressed against our brick façade with her knee in his butt.

"It's just a . . . like, a romantic-squabble kind of thing," I started to say, but I was glad that the cops didn't even look at me. They had Nick's ID out of his wallet in no time, then he was in the cop car while they checked it. I leaned against the brick wall waiting for them to find those warrants Abby had mentioned. The new green paint on the door was scratched to shit.

In the park across the street, the tree branches were frothy with fresh leaves and birds. Behind a window nearby, an old lady watched, half hidden by her curtain.

When the cops left with Nick, I pounded on the door myself, throwing all my tension and anger into it.

"Are they gone?" Skip cracked the door and I shoved my way in.

"I can't believe you locked me out!"

"He didn't hurt you," Skip said.

"No thanks to you! Jesus, I can't believe you wanted to

make Abby go out there! She would have gotten killed!"

"Sid," Skip followed me up the stairs, "this is not my fault!"

I turned on him on the second floor. "We're house-mates, Skip, that was so lame."

"But . . ." he stammered, "the safety of the house . . ."

"Mitch would never have—" I began, but the way he threw up his hands in exasperation really pissed me off. "You're just a coward!"

Skip's face pinched up tight, his lips pursed. We stared at each other for a moment, and then I turned and charged up the next flight of stairs, leaving him standing there on the second floor.

I hadn't meant to get personal, but I was too pissed off to apologize. It seemed like I had to do everything now, while everyone else huddled in the house bicker-ing amongst themselves. And anyway, Jimmy was hurt, Abby could be in danger—I had real problems to attend to.

XII

Abby and I went to Nick's apartment that afternoon. I felt uncomfortable being in his house. He had shown himself to be a violent jerk, and I knew it was right to help Abby get her stuff out of there while she could, but her behavior didn't stand up to close inspection either. I stood around not wanting to touch anything. Abby was totally at home—she helped herself to juice from the fridge and used Nick's phone to call the police and found out that he'd been booked and would be held for a few weeks.

"How do you already have so many clothes?" I loitered in the doorway and watched Abby shove things into garbage bags. "You just lost everything. I have, like, two pairs of jeans."

"I know, it's crazy. I get stuff at work. Do you like this hat?" She put on a fedora from the dresser. "Nick said it looked better on me."

"It's his?"

She saw the expression on my face in the mirror and put it back. She knew what I was thinking: How does a tough squatter girl get mixed up with a thug like Nick?

"I never should have moved in here, it was stupid,"

she said, looking embarrassed. "I was going to move in with Meg and them downtown. You heard they got a loft in Chinatown? It didn't even have a kitchen—they're building everything themselves and it's $500 a month. Each! I don't even want to stay in New York. So Nick was like, *Stay with me*. Then he gets all psycho."

She pulled her hair back from her face and I saw the vulnerability she hid with bravado. Maybe if I had guys offering me nice free places to live, I'd make stupid decisions too.

"Hey, let's call Raven," I suggested. What Abby had told me last night had made me worry. Rot-Squat had been Raven's life; she was so ungrounded now, even her best friend Abby hadn't seen her in a while.

I dialed the number Abby had for Raven's friend on Orchard Street but an irate lady hung up on me.

"She was supposed to be there all month." Abby stood in the doorway, chewing her lip ring. I could see she had a bad feeling like I did. "Try Serenity House."

Raven sounded so distraught when we finally got her on the phone that Abby and I "borrowed" Nick's car keys and headed to the Lower East Side to get her. Abby couldn't drive stick and I was so out of practice and focused on stopping at lights and not stalling out that I almost drove right by Raven, even though she was waiting on Avenue D right where we'd said. I didn't recognize her. Raven's normally tan face was sallow and puckered up, she was yelling at a stocky kid with a pit bull.

I hit the brakes and Abby opened her door. Raven was saying, "I am not a traitor!"

"Taking money from the city," the kid mumbled. "Sellout shit."

"Fuck off, Marky!" Abby said. "Leave her alone."

I took Raven's bag from her, threw it in the car, and helped her climb over Abby's seat.

"What was that?" I asked Raven when we were all in.

Raven put her head in her hands. "I get blamed for everything. There were twenty-four of us there! Everyone knows I'm working with the lawyer, so now it's, like, all my fault . . . but shouldn't we all be doing that?"

"You're doing a good job!" I said. It was heartbreaking how frazzled she looked.

"He got in my face saying I'm trying to take all the money for myself and screw people!"

Abby rolled her eyes. "Marky's on dust."

"I bet he's the one who did that graffiti about me!"

"I heard that was Lee," Abby said.

"What, because we couldn't add him to the list of house residents? Jesus! It was too late!"

"And he didn't live there. Everyone's jealous," Abby said. "Those kids act like we won the lottery."

"But we got screwed! We lost our house! Did they forget already?"

"New York sucks, I'm so over it. It's a yuppie wasteland now anyways." Abby glared out the window like she wanted to punch the city in the face. "Let the rich assholes have it."

I peered at Raven in the rearview, she was scratching at her face. "You want to eat something?"

"Ugh, no. I'm queasy. I was staying with Deena and Zig."

"Oh shit," Abby said. "What were those tweekers on?"

"They never sleep, I'm exhausted," Raven moaned. She lay down with her head on her backpack and her knees curled into her chest.

"You were supposed to be taking it easy at your friend's apartment," Abby said. "What happened?"

"I let Jess stay there with me," Raven's voice cracked, "with Rathead."

"That dog is going to kill someone."

"I know," Raven said. "It would have been okay but then Stumps came over, and then Gibby. They always rile him up."

"Shit."

"Yeah. My friend's cat got bit. We didn't have any money for the vet or anything. It was pretty bad."

"And you got kicked out."

"Whatever." Raven sat up again. "The fleas were totally not our fault! Rathead got them there. The super's being a dick."

"Okay, relax," I said. "We're out of there." We were already on the bridge, lifting up above the dismal gray city. I waved a hand over the steering wheel. "Look: Brooklyn."

* * *

Raven slept in my bed for three days straight. When she finally got up she was slow and quiet and didn't want to leave the neighborhood, so in the evenings after work I started showing her stuff near the Bakery—the bodega with the best sandwiches, the pay phones that didn't eat quarters, and the trash cans at the park across the street where we threw out our poop in plastic bags. In Manhattan, squatters without plumbing in their buildings used bathrooms in cafés and bars. Brooklyn was too residential for that. Our only real toilet was on Lorenzo's floor. But Raven was enthusiastic about our plastic bag system. It reminded her of how you crouched over a hole in India where she'd lived as a kid. She said it cleaned out your colon better than sitting. She said we should make anti-toilet stickers and we laughed ourselves silly drawing stick figures for the logo: *Squatters for squatting.*

The weekend was really hot, and I took Raven down to Kent Avenue where we climbed under the fence past the trash pile to the hidden, disintegrating pier. She spread her arms wide to encompass the city floating over the dark river.

"This is so rad!" she cried. "In the city there'd be a gazillion yuppies walking their dogs here."

I'd been here alone a bunch and always thought how great it would be to show someone who would appreciate it. Raven kicked off her sandals and dangled her feet over the water and we let the river breeze send goose bumps over our sweaty skin.

When we got up again, I led her south past the

burnt-sugar smolder of the Domino factory on the river and past the building Lorenzo and I had called the Chimney. It was still empty. Probably no one had been in it since he and I had spent the night there a year ago. Raven and I walked under the monstrous echoing bridge to the abandoned train-car diner on Wythe. I loved how little it looked under the looming bridge, like a toy train. The old sign that read *Stacy's* had fallen off and was leaning against a window. Raven said we should squat it and start an anarchist-collective café. Which would be great if there were any anarchists around. The area was all Hasidic Jews to the south and Latino families to the north. But it was nice to hear Raven full of crazy ideas, like her old self.

She was wearing an army cap of Abby's over her shaggy grown-out hair and a tank top that I hadn't recognized at first. On me it was a tight undershirt, but it hung loose and relaxed over her thin shoulders. Raven hadn't brought much with her to Brooklyn, but she just went through Abby's stuff or mine and put on whatever she felt like. She'd grown up on an ashram and the concept of private property was pretty hazy for her. I didn't mind, I thought this must be what it would be like having a sister.

We stopped at a bodega for something to drink, and when we walked out, Raven flicked her pierced tongue at me naughtily and lifted the hem of the tank top. She had a box of brownie mix tucked in her shorts.

"You're so bad! We don't even have an oven!"

"You have a toaster oven, right? It'll totally work."

The vision charmed me—girlfriends baking brownies at a sleepover—but when we got back to the Bakery we found that the pan that fit in the toaster oven was too disgusting to use.

"Crust Factory is right!" Raven joked.

I was embarrassed. The kitchen had been nice when Mitch was around. Jimmy never cleaned anything and I'd gotten lazy too. I couldn't even wash out a pan because I hadn't gotten water in days. I wanted Brooklyn to look good to Raven.

"Let's go clean this stuff at the hydrant and get water," I said. I hurried to find buckets and loaded them with dirty dishes and soap and cleaning brushes.

It was dark out but there was a streetlight near the hydrant. Raven and I filled the buckets and got everything soaking in water.

"It's so weird that there's a highway in the middle of the city," Raven mused, her eyes flicking back and forth, following the cars on the BQE. "Where does it go?"

"Queens, I guess."

"To Coney Island?"

"I don't know, I've never been."

"Let's hitchhike there."

"Hey!" A cry made us look up the dark street. Jimmy steered his bike down the middle of Rodney, standing up on the pedals, with Abby perched behind him on the seat, her arms waving. They were dressed like twins in black jeans and tank tops. Jimmy swerved to the curb and Abby tumbled off the bike into the weeds next to us. Raven sprinkled water on her. Abby kicked and squealed.

"What the hell you doing?" Jimmy asked me.

"The dishes." I held up a pan. "What did you cook in this? Cement?"

"Didn't anyone tell you it's Saturday night?"

"I want to do dishes!" Abby leaned over the bucket, happy and drunk. "Gimme a scrubby!"

After Jimmy went back to the house, Raven and Abby lost interest in scrubbing, but they kept me company. They sat in the weeds by the off-ramp and talked about people I didn't know. Occasionally a car careened off the highway heading for Metropolitan Avenue, passing close enough to touch. My converse and shorts and T-shirt got completely soaked but the air was so hot the water felt good.

"We should put patio furniture out here," Abby said. "This could be our garden!"

"We could do that on the roof too," I said. "Have you guys been up there yet?"

"No! That's where that ladder in the kitchen goes?"

"Yeah. It gets really hot up there."

"We could make a solar oven!" Raven clapped her hands. "We just need metal scraps and some glass. Then we could bake our own bread."

We asked Abby about Coney Island and she knew all about it. She said we could ride bikes there, we could take mushrooms and ride the roller coaster and sleep on the beach and swim after dark. I felt giddy with excitement. A part of me zoomed up into the Brooklyn sky and looked down and saw me there with my girlfriends on the highway off-ramp, making plans, and saw how my weirdo misfit squat could actually become the New York home I'd dreamed of.

And it really was. It stayed hot and we rode our bikes to Sweetwater and we went to parties and shows and Stumps started calling us the Three Musketeers because Jimmy worked nights and Raven and Abby and I went everywhere together. A guy Raven was sleeping with drove us all upstate one night and we went swimming in a lake at dawn and slept in the woods.

The best night of all was when Fugazi played. I knew the opening band and they put the three of us on the list and gave us beer from backstage. Everyone I knew in New York was there and everyone was excited and happy. Fugazi were amazing and they must have played for two hours—it went on and on and no one wanted them to stop ever; it wasn't an aggressive pit at all, you could really dance, we kept going until sweat poured off our heads like we'd been swimming.

When we left, a bunch of us rode our bikes up onto the Williamsburg Bridge and sat there drinking beer and looking down at the river. Everything that came out of my mouth was funny and smart. Lorenzo rode by on his way home from the show, and when he saw us, he stopped. I introduced him to the kids he didn't know and then he sat next to me and pointed up the river.

"What's that?" he asked.

"Queensboro Bridge," I said.

And he grinned at me like, *See how far we've come?* I gave him my beer; I didn't even need it.

XIII

One night on our way home from dinner at the L Café, Raven told me she'd been coming up with an idea for a project. She wanted to make portraits of every single squatter she knew in their spaces.

"Now I wish I'd taken more pictures of Rot Squat, you know? None of this is going to last." She clapped her hands. "I can start with you!"

She skipped while she talked, she was excited, so I said, "Sure," even though I hated having my picture taken. I always looked stupid.

Raven herded me into Jimmy's empty room. She found Abby's makeup bag and dumped it out on his bed next to me. She brushed powder onto my face and pushed my hair into place with mousse. I shut my eyes and enjoyed the feel of her hands on my skin. It made me think of Halloween. I was always a man for Halloween— GI Joe, Indiana Jones. All the adults must have been sure I was a lesbian.

Raven got me in place against the brick wall in the kitchen. She set up her camera on a tripod and put a lamp from my room on the floor. She looked through the lens and I tried to appear relaxed, but I didn't remember how people stood. Lean against the wall? Hands on hips? It all felt wrong.

"Sorry," I said awkwardly.

"Let's put on some music," Raven said and went over to the boom box.

That was better. I sang along, making faces.

"Nice!" Raven laughed and took some pictures. I walked like an Egyptian across the wall.

A voice made us both jump. "Do you want to both get in the picture?" I dropped my arms. It was Skip, halfway up the stairs with his hair pulled back in a tight ponytail.

I'd been avoiding him for weeks. Ever since I'd called him a coward that time, I'd felt bad. But the longer I didn't apologize and he didn't mention it, the more impossible it seemed to bring up. "Raven's just taking some pictures," I said.

"Well, I can help." He took a couple steps toward us and held out his hand for the camera. Raven put her hands over it like she wanted to protect it.

"We're just goofing off," I said.

Skip cleared his throat. "You could use the second-floor space for this," he said to Raven. "I don't know if Sid has told you, but we keep that space open for art projects."

"What, we're not allowed to take pictures up here?" she asked.

"Oh, I didn't mean . . . No, art is really good to do here, we just have space for it, I mean."

Raven fiddled with her camera. "*Art*," she mumbled.

"I'm just, like, taking some pictures." I wanted Skip to leave but instead it was Raven who slouched away. She headed over to the kitchen table.

"Raven's just getting going on a thing," I explained, like I had to translate between the two of them. "So, what's up, Skip?"

"If I'm not interrupting, I wanted to ask you something."

He *was* interrupting—Raven was slipping away. "You want to do more, Raven?" I called out to her. But she was already at Jimmy's door.

"Nah, I'm gonna lie down."

Skip settled at the table and leaned toward me. "I'm having a hard time on the street."

"The street?" I was distracted. Raven had been sleeping in my room all month. I shouldn't have said we were just goofing around; I must have offended her.

"You know, where I sell books?" Skip went on. "My friend and I *always* set up on this one corner, we've been there for months, it's our *spot*. Then this person muscled in, a real bully, and there wasn't room and my friend gave up and left but I can't go where he is. So now I'm stuck alone and I mean, we have to help each other out there, you know, watch out for each other, for like thieves and taking bathroom breaks, and I can't even open my mouth, everything I say gets totally attacked . . ."

"Why not get Eddie to help you? Or Lorenzo?"

"It's a little . . ." Skip fidgeted. "I don't want to tell them."

"Uh-huh." I stared at Jimmy's door, listening for movement. What was Raven doing? When Skip left, I'd go in and check on her.

"I just thought if you came by and talked to her . . ."

"Her?" I almost laughed, but when I focused on Skip I saw how tortured his face looked.

"I just think if she saw I had a friend like you . . . I just think you could talk to her . . ."

"Really? What would that do?"

"Please, Sid, it would mean a lot to me."

"Okay, okay." I didn't know what the hell I was going to say to some scary street-hawker lady, but Skip wasn't budging until I agreed. I promised to come by the next week when I had time and he left fast like he was worried I'd change my mind. When he was gone, I walked to Jimmy's door and lifted my hand to knock, but it was so still in there I had second thoughts. Maybe Raven was sleeping or maybe she just wanted to be alone. I didn't want to be pushy, so I dropped my hand and tip-toed away.

"Is that your house?" Laure's perfumed hair swung over my shoulder when she leaned over my sketchbook. It was a quiet afternoon at the dungeon and I was working on my ideas for fixing up the third floor. Donny had told me about a loft bed a guy he knew was giving away. We were going to get it tonight and I was planning to set it up for Raven by the kitchen. If I hung sheets under the loft she could have a private dressing room and desk down there—her own space. Then she'd want to stay.

"It's so amazing you know how to build stuff! Kathy, you have to see Sid's drawings!" Laure called.

Kathy clicked across the floor and kicked off her heels, like she always did when she wanted to concentrate. She flipped through the pages of my sketchbook. "Very nice," she murmured. "Excellent." I drew all kinds of things, but I'd especially loved drawing houses ever since I was a little kid and we moved to a new apartment or trailer every year. I drew fantastical floor plans, chains of rooms that snaked on forever, hidden courtyards, towers, secret stairways.

"You have a lot of windows, the space must be beautiful," Kathy mused over the last page. I'd drawn the whole floor, thinking about where we could put a darkroom for Raven someday too, and build walls for a living room around the woodstove so it would be easier to heat.

"I could never be a squatter," Laure sighed. "I don't know how to do *anything*."

"You know how to do stuff!" I laughed. "Your clients love you!"

"Oh, *that*."

"Seriously, I always wondered how you got the kitty cat man out of the bathroom that time."

"When Alison couldn't get him out?" Laure smirked. "She just kept *scolding* him."

"Isn't that what he was here for?"

"The playacting can be intimidating. Sometimes a guy gets stage fright. So I told him I knew he looked sexy in the cat suit and I wanted to see him."

"That's it?"

Laure shrugged.

"Never underestimate flattery," Kathy said. "Or the delicacy of the male ego."

"I should use that more on my housemates."

"Why, what's going on?" Laure asked. She and Kathy loved hearing squat stories.

"I told you about how Eddie and Skip didn't get it when Abby's boyfriend was flipping out. They wanted to throw her out there to get killed—they're so clueless. Anyways, I caught Skip eavesdropping on us the other night. Can you believe that? I left my room to get something and I bumped right into him in the dark. It scared the crap out of me."

"He must be in love with one of you," Laure said.

"I don't think that's it. He hates couples."

"Girl talk," Kathy said. "He feels left out, inferior."

"It's so nice there're finally girls around!"

"Sure, but you've just been one of the guys, right? Now there's this little bonbon swishing around, changing partners. It upsets the balance."

Laure grabbed my arm like I was about to fall over. "You've got to talk to him!"

Donny and I went to his friend's place in Red Hook that night and broke down the loft bed. We hauled the pieces into Donny's truck and then drove back to the Bakery.

The next day was Saturday and I got up early all excited to get the thing put together. Raven hadn't come back from the city last night. She was taking pictures and using a friend's darkroom. She said being in Brooklyn made her more creative; there was more space out here, more time.

I needed to cut down two of the loft legs to make them match but the only saw I could find was an old rusty hand saw Mitch had left. It was pretty slow going.

Jimmy came out of his room at some point in a Bad Religion shirt to use the piss bucket in the closet. "Morning!" I called, but he just grunted.

Abby came out behind him, yawning. "Wow, look at all that!" She stretched. "Need help?"

"Yes," I said, "I can't remember how this all goes together."

Jimmy walked back through to the bedroom. "I thought we were going to Lucky's."

"We can head over there later, can't we? I'm going to put on some jeans." She went into their room and Jimmy shut the door behind her.

"We were supposed to be there at eleven," I heard Jimmy whine. I put a CD in my boom box so I didn't have to listen to them.

"Is this for your friend?" Skip asked, making me jump. I hadn't heard him arrive over the music.

"Raven? Well . . ." I stalled. I didn't want him to think I was moving people into the house without discussing it with him. "It's just, like, for guests. You know, we have so much space."

The song ended, and I could hear Abby and Jimmy weren't bickering anymore; there was a muffled squeal and a groan. Jimmy's bed creaked. Did Skip hear that too?

"Do you want some help? You need a power saw?" Skip asked.

"I'm okay."

"Who was that guy here yesterday?"

"You mean Donny? He's my friend I used to work for, I told you about him."

"I thought maybe he was moving in."

"Nope." Was Skip messing with me? "Just helping out."

"You're coming by next week, right?"

"I said I would." I pounded a bolt into the wood where the leg connected to the loft frame. Why wouldn't it go in? I hoped Skip would see I was busy and clear out, but he meandered around with his hands in his pockets looking out the windows at the rain. A moan escaped from Jimmy's room.

"You remember the address, right?" Skip asked.

I glanced up and hit my finger with the hammer. "Ouch! Crap!" Tears of pain popped into my eyes.

"You all right?" Skip sprang toward me. "Is it bad?"

"It's fine," I said. "Jesus! Just let me concentrate!"

I ran into my room and threw myself on my bed. Skip shuffled around outside my door but I willed him to leave. It really hurt and it was his fault for distracting me. Finally he left. I considered getting ice for my finger but then Jimmy and Abby trooped by my door and down the stairs, discussing how to get to their friend's place, without so much as a *See you later*—and I decided to just stay in bed.

Later I stopped feeling sorry for myself and got the loft built. It was done by the time Raven came back after dark. She loved it; she got settled in and everything was fine for a couple days. Then I got home at the end of the week and found Abby in my bedroom. She was writing a letter, her long bare legs swung over the side of my easy chair.

"What's up?" I dropped my messenger bag on the floor.

"Your buddy Skip's in my room," she shrugged. "So I came in here."

"Why? What's he doing?"

She rolled her eyes. "I think it's, like, a nonviolent sit-in? Seriously. You should check it out."

I walked across the third floor. Jimmy's door was open and there was Skip on the floor between the open window and the unmade bed, cross-legged, tracing patterns on the wood floor with a finger. His short-sleeved red shirt made him look like a clerk at RadioShack.

"What's going on?" I asked.

"It's my house," he said to the floorboards. "I can go anywhere I want."

"Other people's rooms?"

"It's *not her room!*" He tapped the floor with each word.

"It's Jimmy's room. He can have guests if he wants!"

"*We* used to be his guests. *We* used to hang out up here."

He was giving me a meaningful look, like he was trying to remind me of something important, but I couldn't remember Skip ever hanging out with Jimmy. They'd always been oil and water, Skip so serious and Jimmy making jokes about everything.

"Well, talk to your pal Jimmy then," I said sarcastically. "Invite him out for a beer! But don't go barging into other people's rooms!"

"Why not? It's my house."

"God, Skip, don't be so dense! Don't you understand a woman could feel threatened? What if she was changing or something?"

"I don't want to look at her!" Skip protested, and stood up. "That's crazy! It's a squat! I . . . I used to live in a corner with a sheet up!"

"Well, at this squat," I said with exaggerated patience, "we have our own rooms and we respect each other's privacy."

"No one cares about privacy until they're *mating.*" Skip held his hands out like he couldn't believe I was being so dense. I stared back, arms crossed. His expression changed. He leaned back and considered me critically. "You didn't come by."

"Skip, what the hell can I do? I'm going to talk to some lady I don't even know and . . . what? What? Tell me what that's going to do."

He looked at me like I was pathetic, which was nuts. He was the one barging into Jimmy and Abby's room, asking me to come solve his stupid social problems. *He* was the weirdo. But he shook his head all disappointed, like he was giving up on me, and went downstairs.

When Jimmy and Raven got home later, they sat on my bed next to Abby and I sat above them on my chair and told them about Skip. I was feeling strange about the whole thing, like I was somehow in the wrong, and I guess because that seemed unfair I made Skip sound even worse than he was. But Jimmy just looked bored and said, "This house has bad vibes."

"Oh my god." Raven hugged my pillow. "Maybe someone died in the fire!"

"What fire?"

"When this building used to be a bakery! There was a fire and the building got abandoned, right?" She peered around wide-eyed. "That's why they didn't rebuild!"

"Creepy!" Abby nestled cozily next to Jimmy.

"We should get a shaman to come do a cleanse," Raven said.

"A *cleanse*?" Jimmy laughed.

"We had to do that in a house where I lived upstate," Abby said. "It was totally haunted by this girl who drowned in the pond and we got this lady to come and she burned sage and did this chanting . . ."

"Do you know how to find her?"

"What do we care?" Jimmy tweaked Abby. "We're leaving."

Everyone got quiet and no one looked at me.

"Leaving?" I echoed.

Abby played with a patch on Jimmy's jacket and avoided my eyes.

"*California über alles*," Jimmy sang.

"Both of you?"

"We can't stay here," Abby said. "Nick's getting out of jail soon . . ."

"And then if Skip's gonna get all whack . . ." Jimmy shrugged.

"We can talk to Skip, he's not so bad!" I shouldn't have complained about him like that. "Skip just . . . he had really weird parents."

"Who didn't?" Jimmy responded.

"Like, he told me this story how when he was in first grade he was the only kid who went to school on Halloween with no costume. His parents just totally blew it off."

They all looked at me blankly.

"Weird, right? And the teacher tried to get something together for him before the parade, so she had him up by her desk wrapping him in brown paper to be, like, a tree, and she was super upset. He saw she was upset and then he knew something was really wrong . . ." When Skip had told me this story, he'd told it flat, without affect at all, but it had made me hollow with loneliness. I felt it now too, but everyone stared at me like they were waiting for the punch line.

"A lot of people have worse shit than no Halloween costume," Abby said.

"But . . . he's up in front of his whole class, crying. It's humiliating."

"When I was little I saw a kid get run over," Raven said. "He lost both his feet."

"Like Ricky Vee! Train hopping. You know that dude?" Abby said.

"Oh god," Raven replied, "I haven't seen him in ages—"

"Anyways," Jimmy cut in, "we're going to California. My parents're giving us their old station wagon. Baby blue, fake wood paneling, AM radio . . ."

"Rad," Raven said.

I felt devastated that Jimmy and Abby were leaving; did she really not care?

"Did you guys know Stumps is squatting this old theater in Brooklyn with a bunch of people?" Raven said. "It sounds really cool."

"But . . . what's wrong with here?" I blurted. *What about the loft I just built for you?* I wanted to scream.

"Sid, seriously," Raven said, "come check this place out, it sounds amazing. There's a stage and we can do shows and have a gallery and café, it's huge! It was a theater!"

"Who else is involved?" Abby asked.

"You know those German DJs who were staying at ABC? They want to do raves there."

"I love those guys!" Abby cried. "Remember that party at the Frying Pan when they wore those helmets?"

Raven remembered, and Jimmy remembered, and I remembered too, but all the fun stuff we'd done this summer seemed meaningless now. Tomorrow was the first of September—it was going to be winter before we knew it. It was time to make plans and settle in, and instead it felt like everything was falling apart.

XIV

Stumps led us from the Bakery into East Williamsburg. I never went this direction when I explored. I liked the romantic empty warehouses on the North Side. Over here it was all apartment buildings, souped-up cars, and gangs of Latino kids looking for trouble.

We sloped down Lorimer Street into a valley of housing projects. At the bottom of the hill, the elevated subway loomed over Broadway, where there were suddenly more people, dollar stores, a McDonald's. Stumps paused. "Check 'er out."

Past the Food Town parking lot was a sandstone mansion, pale and square. The first-floor windows were bricked up and on the second and third floors huge arched frames were glassless, open to the elements.

When we got up to it we found the front door propped open with a cinder block. Stumps pushed in and we followed. To the left was a gaping chasm of black: a dark room rank with mattresses and garbage. But in the high stairwell where we were, a round window illuminated a marble staircase missing half its treads.

"This is beautiful," I breathed through the sleeve of my shirt. My feet stuck to the floor.

"What's the stench?" Abby choked behind me.

"Human shit, my friends," Stumps said. "Come on."

He scaled up the iron framework of the stairs. It was sturdy, the missing treads would be easy to replace with wood. On the second floor, a door from the wide hallway led into a giant room surrounded by the floor-to-ceiling windows we'd seen from outside.

"So cool!" Raven gasped.

Stumps looked smug. "Wait till you see upstairs."

"What's the deal with this place?" I asked. "Did you find out who owns it?"

"Yeah, I went downtown," he said. The stairs to the next floor were almost intact. "It's registered to some company in the Bahamas. But they're behind on taxes."

"Can you squat something that's privately owned?"

"Well, the squats are all owned by the city because the owners didn't pay taxes, right?" said Raven. "So this is the same thing. Or will be soon."

"Obviously the owner doesn't care," Abby agreed. "I mean, look at this."

On the third floor a door led into an airy room with a ceiling so high it looked at first like there was no roof at all, just air. The floor was wood plank, wide and empty. Abby and Raven raced each other to the center of the room and threw themselves into a tango on the small stage under the domed skylight. Around the perimeter of the space was a balcony trimmed with tin wainscoting.

Raven dipped Abby and they stumbled and shrieked.

Stumps and I clapped. "Imagine bands playing here!" I said. "At ABC No Rio they play in a *basement!*"

"Imagine, Sid," Raven called, twirling on the stage, "we can choose who lives here, just the people we love!"

The people we love. Like me. I was excited. I climbed a narrow flight of stairs up to the balcony and Stumps followed. At the far end of the balcony, a lump moved and I jumped back. Stumps caught me before I slammed into him. A skinny man in a baseball cap sat up, shoving aside a filthy blanket.

The guy got to his feet, keeping his eyes on the floor, and scurried past us, toward the stairs. We heard the hall door slam, echoing in the silent room.

Stumps poked a toe at the wool blanket the guy had been sitting on. A vial rolled across the floor. "Smokin' the crack pipe, yo."

Abby and Raven joined us on the balcony, wide-eyed and subdued. "So, is it, like, squatted already?" Abby whispered.

"The door isn't secured," I pointed out.

"There's definitely folks crashing here. Especially down on that first floor," Stumps said. "But it's just transients, people looking for somewhere to shoot up and turn tricks."

"They can find someplace else," I said. This building was too special to be used like that. The potential! At least four bedrooms on the first and second floors; a collectively run venue upstairs, a café, a gallery, meeting space. Now the Bakery seemed limited and small and compromised by my clueless housemates. This was a million times better.

"Crap," Raven said when we crested the hill with our camping packs and saw the morning sun hitting the sandstone façade of the Theater. It was three weeks later and the day had arrived. "That's Lee's truck."

"I thought he was at 5th Street now."

"He's such a jerk. Maybe they're already sick of him too."

We were here at nine a.m., just like we'd agreed, but Lee and his friends had a generator on the sidewalk already. Stumps burst out of the Theater and rubbed Raven's fuzzy head affectionately.

There were people behind Stumps, people leaning out of the second-floor windows, people on the roof, people speaking in excited voices in the staircase.

"Where do we start?" one of the German DJs in baggy pants and steel glasses asked Stumps.

Stumps handed them a broom from the back of Lee's van. "Let's get the stairwell cleaned up."

"The girls can do that." Lee grabbed the broom and shoved it at Raven without even looking at us. "You two go look at the drainpipe on the roof. It's clogged and pouring water down the south wall."

Lee's long dreads were tied back with a bandanna and he was wearing Carhartt overalls on top of a wife-beater exposing massive shoulders and arms. The Germans went up the stairs as directed, but Raven shied toward the door, ignoring the broom.

"We brought garbage bags," she told Stumps, "Me and Sid're going to get the second floor cleaned up."

"Rad." Stumps smiled wide, compensating for Lee's rudeness.

"You see what I mean," Raven said upstairs. "Lee makes everything totally not fun. I can't believe Stumps brought him here without even telling us."

"We can still have fun," I said, but she just sighed. "Let's start with the broken glass. We can put it in this box." Raven and I thought the second floor was where bedrooms should be built first. It wasn't as gross as the pitch-dark first floor, where the windows were bricked up and the ground was covered in scabby old mattresses and human waste, or as wide open as the third floor.

Soon Stumps came up and Raven asked, "What's Lee doing here?"

"He wants to live here," Stumps answered.

"Why?"

"Lee has trouble with the city, you know. Too many people. He thinks being out here in Brooklyn'll be better."

"Lucky for us." Raven glared at Stumps until he headed upstairs to check on the Germans.

Footsteps and voices echoed in the marble stairwell.

"There're a lot of people here," Raven said.

"Stumps told us we'd need a lot of people to fix the place up."

"Yeah, I shouldn't worry. Hardly anyone's going to want to live way out here in bumfuck Brooklyn when it comes down to it." She didn't sound very enthusiastic herself.

Raven and I had been so excited about this place. We'd brought sleeping bags so we could stay a few days and establish ourselves as house members. We'd agreed we'd take turns going back to the Bakery and making it look like we were still living there, so that we wouldn't raise any suspicions with my housemates until we saw if this place would really work out. But I was sure it would, this building was amazing. The floor-to-ceiling arched windows gave Raven and me a wide view of the parking lot of the grocery store, the housing projects in the distance, Broadway under the elevated train. I could see below on the sidewalk where Lee and his buddies had pulled the front door off. They were pouring concrete to fix the stoop and repairing the frame so it would be secure. Their tools were scattered all over the sidewalk. A cop car pulled up and I leaned out the window holding my breath.

"Afternoon," Stumps called, jumping to the curb like a friendly doorman.

"Afternoon," the officer riding shotgun said. "Anybody bothering you folks? You need anything?"

"No sir," Stumps saluted. "So far so good."

The officer waved and the car cruised around the corner.

Raven leaned out the window next to me. "*Need anything?*" she laughed in amazement.

Stumps spread his arms out like he'd just performed a magic trick, and bowed.

Voices brought us back to the window awhile later. Stumps was talking to a tiny thin woman with dark hair piled on her head and sunglasses and a laundry cart.

"We work for this construction company the owner hired," he was telling her, the cover story we'd agreed on. "We're fixing the place up."

"What's going to happen?" she asked.

"They don't tell us much," Stumps said. "We're just supposed to clean it up and keep the riffraff out."

"Keep the people out who've been using it?" Her voice was loud for a small lady.

Stumps shrugged and smiled.

"What right do you have?" her voice shot up.

"Um, well, like I said . . . we work for—"

"You don't look like construction workers." She backed away, eyeing Stumps's spiked vest, tattoos. Her laundry cart hit the curb. Stumps jumped to catch it from falling and she screamed, "Get away from me!"

Stumps froze. I saw her face now, as she backed across the street, twisted, missing teeth.

She joined two men I hadn't noticed waiting at the fence. They were skinny like her, not young. They looked up at the second floor, right at Raven and me, and we flinched away from the window.

"We're, like, the *cops*," Raven said.

"They're just . . . *junkies* . . ." I said.

"Yeah," she agreed, "and we're just dirty squatters."

* * *

In the evening, Lee and Stumps sat on the stage upstairs with the rest of us scattered around the empty, dusty floor. Everyone agreed the building had to stay occupied at all times, but hardly anyone was prepared to actually sleep over tonight. Raven and I had made beds for ourselves on the second floor. Stumps and Lee and some sullen boys with face tattoos and a pit bull were going to sleep up in the balcony. The Germans said they would come back tomorrow. Everyone else was silent.

Raven finally spoke up: "What about all the people who were using this place before us? I feel bad excluding them."

"*Excluding* them?" Lee's eyebrows shot up.

"They were here first," Raven said. "So like—"

"You're kidding me." Lee put his head in his hands. "I am so sick of talking about the fucking junkies."

"But . . ." Raven looked around for support. I sat up straight but I didn't know what to say.

"Raven, hey, listen," Stumps said, hunched over his crossed legs, "we've been discussing this, and believe me, we take it super serious—"

"You want to give a bunch of junkies keys to the place," Lee's raised voice cut him off. "So all the work we've just done cleaning up after them—they can just shit on it again. That's what you want?"

"I don't . . . I just meant . . ."

"If you don't know what you want, why bring it up?" Lee looked around. "You feel bad? You want a hug, maybe? Can someone give Raven a hug so we can move on?" People shifted and looked at the ground.

"Are there other compromises we could talk about?" I said, but my voice was thin and Lee talked over me.

"The one thing we have to offer the neighborhood is getting this place cleaned up. We get rid of the junkies. We get rid of the prostitutes. That's how we make friends with the neighborhood. End of story."

"What neighbors? The grocery store? The J train?" Raven stepped backward, toward the door. She was so small, with her big eyes and cropped hair, she looked like a child in the large room.

Lee's lip curled. "Anyone who can't handle the reality here should leave."

"The junkies *are* the neighbors," Raven said on her way out the door.

Downstairs, Eli and Lydia stopped to say goodbye to Raven and me. Whenever I ran into them, I thought of their room at Rot-Squat, of Mitch and me bickering about the *Star Wars* figures.

Eli squatted on his haunches by where Raven and I sat on our sleeping bags. "This is Rot-Squat all over again." He shook his head dismally like that was a bad thing, which surprised me. Rot-Squat had always looked like a big cozy family to me.

"It's the court case." Raven rolled her eyes. "Lee's so pissed that the rest of us might get money."

"He should have thought of that before he was beating his housemates with a bat!" Lydia said. She darted a nervous look over her shoulder, like Lee might be there. They were leaving anyway. They'd come to check it out and help today, but they weren't impressed. They had a lead on a loft in Long Island City. They both worked; they were going to give up and pay rent.

When we were alone, Raven said, "We should ditch out too. This is bullshit."

"Already?" The potential of this building was so enormous; I didn't want to let it go. I was secretly glad hardly anyone was spending the night here. It meant that they weren't serious about the place, that we'd get the good spaces for ourselves. Maybe Raven and I would have the whole second floor. We could have two bedrooms in back, and a lounge and kitchen with a big table where we could serve dinner to our friends under the arched windows.

"Let's see how it plays out," I urged. "If we stick it out we'll have more say in the future. Maybe Lee won't last here if he makes everyone hate him."

"No one from Rot-Squat would have come if they knew he was involved. Stumps was an idiot to trust him."

"Lee did bring the truck," I pointed out. "And tools, and those dudes who work construction with him . . ."

"So he should get his way, then?"

"I didn't say that." A train rattled past, making it too loud to talk. The lights rushed along the wall and over the floor across us. Every light, every mosquito, every passing noise from the street seemed amplified by the huge windows. Raven turned her back to me on her sleeping bag.

As sore and exhausted as my body was from the long day of work, I couldn't sleep. It must always be like this in a new squat: uncomfortable and strange. But hardly anyone I knew had actually squatted an empty building. Most of the squats in the city had been established years ago. Mitch. Only Mitch. I wished I could ask him if he had ever dealt with this kind of thing. What would he do? I felt sure he was in Maine, but I didn't have his address and I knew he didn't have a phone on the island. He'd said the closest town was called Brooklin. I wondered if I could look him up somehow—call information. Call the police. I pictured talking to the town sheriff, who would look like Andy Griffith. He'd paddle out to Mitch's island to get him. Mitch, in plaid flannel, would be busy chopping firewood. He would race into town thinking someone had died. *Hey, stranger*, I'd say at the end of the line. Maybe he'd laugh with relief when he heard my voice. Maybe he'd be pissed off.

I must have dozed off because banging on the door startled me awake. Raven was sitting up. I crawled to the window, keeping low to the ground.

Two shady-looking black guys were hitting the new door. "What the fuck? Who's in there?"

They screamed some guy's name. Barry? Harry?

"I'ma kill you, motherfucker!" their hoarse voices sounded terrifyingly close. Could they climb up into this window? They kicked the door. Lee had done his work well, it held on its new hinges. I stayed on the ground until they gave up and left, spitting curses behind them. Then I crawled back to where Raven was curled in a ball.

"They're gone."

"They'll be back," she mumbled into her pillow.

I was wide awake now. I lit my candle again and wondered if I should go upstairs and tell the others.

Raven turned over and stared at the ceiling. "When I was a kid I was embarrassed to be white. When we lived in India. Everyone treated us different. I wanted to be invisible. At least they were nice there. Uganda was worse. I feel really white here."

"It's not like we *have* anything," I said. "We're not rich."

"We can leave. That's our privilege."

I looked around the shadowy room for something to say. "Where else did you live?"

"God, everywhere," she sighed. "Australia one year. Upstate New York. California. My mom grew up in California so I always kind of thought of that as home. She talked about it like home. It's funny, now my dad lives there and she doesn't. He married this rich lady and lives in a big house in Santa Cruz—like, everything I thought he hated. Well, I guess they meditate a lot still."

"Where's your mom?"

"Mexico. My brother's there too."

"I remember. You were going to visit them last winter."

"Yeah. I was going and then Rot-Squat got evicted. You'd think that'd be the perfect time to leave, right? But then I felt like I couldn't."

"I get that."

"I don't even know why I want to be in New York anymore. I was going to be this great photographer but I hated being in school, it was a waste of time. I thought that instead of paying tuition, I'd get more done if I just spent my money on film and darkrooms, you know? But it never works out, I don't know why. There's no time. Everyone's all worked up about stupid shit like where to live. As if it matters. It's so tense. Look at me, yelling at Lee. Everyone's so *angry*."

"It's just a bad night." I lay down on my sleeping bag. My fingers curled around her wrist and squeezed. Her hands had been clenched together and they relaxed. "It'll get better. You're so talented."

"Really?"

"I love your photographs! No one else is documenting this stuff! I even liked your pictures of me, and that means you're amazing. No one takes good pictures of me."

She shut her eyes. Her breathing slowed down. Maybe she slept. I stayed on guard, my whole body alert to the street below, ready for anything.

XV

"You alone here?" After work I found Stumps on a couch someone had dragged up to the second floor and put under the window. His narrow eyes were puffy and dark in his round face.

"Guard shift," he yawned, stretching his tongue piercing out like a cat. "Lee and them went to get some stuff in the city. I can't do anything useful, I'm too tired."

"Me too." I sat next to him and put my feet up on the windowsill.

He took a drink from a Gatorade bottle and then held it up like evidence. "You been to that bodega around the corner? Fuckin' drug front, no joke. They have, like, two old Twinkies on some dusty-ass shelves and four huge dudes behind the counter."

"Shit."

"Yeah. I go in and I'm all like, *Crap, this is weird.* I want to be cool so I grab this instead of running out. It's like, blueberry flavor? Never seen this shit before. And the dudes are looking at me like, *Who's this freak?* and I only had a twenty and they said, *Take it.*"

"Seriously? You didn't pay?"

"Weird, right?" The subway brakes screamed as a

train stopped outside and Stumps's hands flew up automatically to cover his ears, like he'd been doing that all day.

Lee brought a roll of plastic to the Theater the next day and we started stretching it over the big windows on the second floor.

I felt less intimidated by Lee now. Stumps had been telling me all about their history and it made him seem more human. Stumps and Lee had met in Queens when Lee got sent up there from the South because his single mom couldn't handle him. He moved in with an uncle who lived near Stumps's family. They got into exploring abandoned buildings and going to punk shows. In the city they found a way into an empty building and started sleeping there. There had been an older guy squatting up in the attic, a paranoid kind of dude, but they helped him out and finally they made a truce with him and started working on the place and letting other people move in. That became Rot-Squat.

I had my staple gun and I showed Lee a trick I'd learned from Mitch. I tore pieces of cardboard from a box and stapled through them so the plastic didn't tear.

"Smart," Lee said. He started tearing cardboard pieces to hand me and I kept stapling. "She calm down?" he asked, gesturing at the sleeping bags in back of the room.

"Who? Raven?" I stalled because I didn't know how to answer.

"I didn't want her getting the doubts in front of everyone." There was still a bit of Carolina in his voice. And some beseeching. "You gotta shut that down before it sets everyone else off. I figured you'd talk her down."

"She seemed okay this morning." I glanced back at the corner like she could hear us talking about her. I found it hard to believe that Lee's bullying was really a thought-out strategy; it came too naturally. "You know, I agree the junkies have to be locked out." I stared at my hand on the stapler to steady my resolve. "But I also think we can't live here unless we listen to each other."

"Oh, I listen," Lee scoffed. "Then I call bullshit when I see it."

"Okay," I said evenly. "But if I'm going to put a lot of work into a place, I want to know we're going to use consensus to make decisions. I know it can seem like a waste of time to hear someone out when you know they're wrong. But if you don't . . . you don't want people to feel steamrolled. They get frustrated and it's not any fun."

"Fun? Since when are we doing this for fun?"

"Are we doing it 'cause someone's holding a gun to our heads?"

Lee's ironic look made me self-conscious, but now that I had started I kept going. "Fun is kind of important, really. If it's not fun, then what's the point? We have to take care of each other and not let people burn out. Everyone has to feel responsible for decisions or they're not really going to stick to them, you know? So you have to be patient through the part where you reach consensus. If people don't agree they'll just undermine it anyways."

"Okay," Lee said.

I breathed out. I'd been frozen in place. I reached for another piece of cardboard, but Lee was looking at where Raven and I had placed our sleeping bags.

"That where you want to build your room?" he asked. "Let's start on it tomorrow, get it done before it's cold."

The conversation with Lee felt like a triumph. I'd made him listen. Well, we all had the same goals, right? If I could forge a bond with Lee and get some influence over him while coaxing Raven along, maybe I could make this whole thing work. I felt like I could do it, I felt strong and focused. I'd been meaning to call my dad and tell him about the new building and I stopped at the pay phone when I went out to get a burrito on Graham Avenue.

"That's my kid!" my dad laughed. "They're just handing you the buildings now, take your pick!"

"This place is going to be a ton of work, but we've got a good crew."

"Well, since you're queen of New York now, you'll have to give me a tour when I'm there." He was coming for a work event in a couple weeks. I said I'd meet him at his hotel for dinner. It sounded fun; I even felt good about facing Angela. I'd been such a mope last winter when I stayed with them. Everything was different now; they'd see how far I'd come.

* * *

We'd only had enough plastic to cover half the windows, and it didn't actually help much. The banging and cursing occurred nightly. It might have been just one or two guys, but it felt like we were under siege—about to be surrounded and dragged out by a mob with our heads on sticks. On the weekend, bored kids from the projects roamed in packs looking for trouble, and from our windows, Raven and I watched them beat up one of the junkies we'd come to recognize. Then it started raining and everyone disappeared. It got windy and the plastic over the windows ripped and flapped into the room. The third floor leaked everywhere, so it wasn't any better. Raven wouldn't go up there anyway, because of Lee. Instead, she went into the city and didn't come back.

On Sunday I told Stumps I couldn't stay any longer. I had to work during the week and I needed to get some sleep and it was too cold and scary and loud at the Theater.

"Sid, we *need* you. Lee's not coming back till Tuesday but I'll be back tomorrow. If the cops or anyone who's gotta be talked to comes . . ." Stumps nodded upstairs where the sullen dudes with tattoos on their faces were drinking Mad Dog. I still hadn't heard them talk. I didn't want them to be here alone either. If a crisis happened, I didn't trust them to handle it.

"You'll be back tomorrow night?"

"Yes, I swear. Just stay tonight? Lee really trusts you."

I must have stood up straighter or something, because Stumps saw he had me. He put his hand on my shoulder. "Lee said you're solid. He said we need more like you."

When Stumps left, I went upstairs determined to talk to the guys up there. They were my new housemates, after all. I got out of them that they were from Idaho. One guy sort of mumbled strange words under his breath and the other guy snickered and looked at the ground. I felt foolish talking to them, like they were laughing at me. They offered me a joint but I turned it down—this place made me too paranoid already.

I went back downstairs and tried to read. I heard voices on the sidewalk below, metal scratching. Was someone trying to break in? I blew out my candle. Why was it so important that I was in here? I was cold, uncomfortable, bored, scared. This was worth fighting for? Me and the morose dudes upstairs were doing something so great and important? My aspirations seemed silly. I was ready to open the door and scream, *Take this stupid place if you want it so bad!*

After work the next day, I stopped at the Bakery to get clean clothes before going back to the Theater. There was mail for me on the floor of the foyer, a large manila envelope. It had come from Veronica. Before I could open it, I heard voices in Lorenzo's room and paused to listen.

"Do you guys hang out with them? No, right? I didn't

think so!" Skip ranted, so loud and worked up probably none of them had heard me open the door. "And those bitches have *keys* to this *house!* Sid just gives a key to whoever she feels like!"

I'd been ready for a fight for days. I shoved through the curtains into Lorenzo's room, the curtains that I had hung back when this was *my* room. "Is this a house meeting?" I asked. They stared in surprise: Eddie with a cigarette halfway to his mouth, Skip frozen mid-pace. "Am I not invited to house meetings now?"

Lorenzo groaned and fell back on his mattress where he was sitting. "Sid, we just talking, keep it chill."

"I think if Skip has something to say to me, he should say it to my face."

Skip stepped toward me. "Maybe if you were honest with us, Sid, then we would be square with you."

"What are you talking about?" I asked.

"We are *talking* about you moving your *pals* in here without a word to anyone else."

"Abby is staying with Jimmy! Not me!"

"And you're not even here! I asked that tattoo girl where you were yesterday and—"

"Her name," I raised my voice, "is Raven."

"Well, I wouldn't know!" Skip yelled. "She doesn't talk to me! You go in and out with your girly gossip parties like I don't even exist!" His voice cracked. "You don't care about this building anymore, do you?"

"What? Of course I do!"

"Yeah, right!"

"What's that supposed to mean?"

"You're never here! You said you'd come help me and you never came and . . . and," he stood up taller, like he really had me now, "what about your mural?"

"My mural?"

Skip threw his hands in the air, like that beat all. "Your stupid girlfriend has to go. She's out of here!" He shoved past me to the door. "If you love each other so much, you can go too!"

"She's not going anywhere!" I screamed after him.

Eddie ran after Skip and their footsteps pounded up the stairs. Lorenzo just sat there on his bed.

"You're just going to let him do this?" I cried.

"I had it under control," he said. "You get him all *loco*, arguin' an' shit."

"Me? This is *my* fault?"

"Just let him shoot off his mouth. He always gets over it."

"He's up there throwing Raven's stuff on the street and you're not going to do anything?"

"I'm not gettin' in his way." Lorenzo lay back again, hands under his head.

I dashed up the stairs and stopped on the second floor. I could hear Skip and Eddie above me, voices and footsteps. What was I going to do, run up and play tug-of-war with Raven's backpack? I was standing in front of my unfinished mural and I studied it like it would give me a clue. Giuliani as Humpty Dumpty—it wasn't a terrible concept. But I'd only painted in the Mohawked punk kid drinking beer and one of the cops; the rest was just sketched in charcoal, faded and smudged. It looked like crap.

Footsteps rushed back down the stairs and Skip burst onto the floor, his hands empty, face as red as his shirt. He charged past me into his room and slammed the frosted-glass door.

Eddie came behind him slower, and paused when he saw me. "Boy," he shook his head, reaching in his pocket for his tobacco, "I ain't *never* seen Skip like this! You two gots to *talk*."

"Talk? How can I talk to someone who's throwing a fit like a five-year-old?"

Eddie looked at me in disbelief. Or maybe disgust. "Jeez, Sid. You're *cold*." He went to his room and shut the door and I was alone.

Cold? How was all this my fault? I went upstairs and got the clothes I wanted and hurried out of the house. I crossed Rodney Street walking fast. I was next to the basketball court by the highway when it hit me that the whole fight was moot if Abby and Jimmy were taking off and Raven and I were moving to the Theater. Why hadn't I just said that?

I leaned into the chain-link fence. As much as I wanted to believe otherwise, I knew the Theater was never going to be ready for winter. In my excitement about my new friends and new house, I'd been burning my bridges with Skip and Eddie and Lorenzo and not putting work into getting my space at the Bakery ready for another winter. I'd been focusing on the wrong things.

I stared at the empty ball court. It was just over a year ago that I'd played here with Skip and Mitch. I remembered how much hope that game had given me—how much I believed that these oddballs could be my new community. But it was the only game we'd ever played.

I felt sick. I opened my backpack to get my water bottle and saw the envelope from Veronica and tore it open. It was a booklet.

New York City Real Estate: Public Auction, read the title. A note fluttered to the ground but I left it and fumbled through the pages. It was overcast and dusk but I could see enough to know I was looking at pictures of empty houses and lots owned by the city. Donny had told me how Giuliani was trying to get all the abandoned properties back on the tax rolls. And there it was. The Bakery looked unfamiliar in the tiny black-and-white snapshot. To me, the building was a kaleidoscope of people— rooms and spaces with different atmospheres; possibilities and disappointments. How could an inch of printed paper contain our whole world? Were we inside when the picture was taken? What had we been doing?

November 12, it said on the cover. I stooped to pick up Veronica's note.

Bad news, baby. Good thing you've got the new place going.
Call me.

I hardly noticed I'd started walking, like a zombie,

until there I was, almost at the Theater as it started raining again. I stopped at the deli to buy an overpriced tea
in a paper cup and the thought of my tidy kitchen at the
Bakery, the one Mitch had built, made me want to cry.
I didn't even have a hot plate at the Theater because
we didn't have electricity. Stumps had gotten Ivor from
9th Street Squat out here—he'd worked at Con Ed and
helped all the squats out—but he said something was
wrong with our fuse box. It was a bigger problem that
we weren't close to figuring out.

The guys from Idaho were waiting for me at the
Theater looking antsy. They left as soon as I came in.
Stumps wasn't back yet. I sat upstairs huddled with my
tea looking at the auction booklet with my flashlight.
Twenty-four thousand was the starting bid. I guess that
wasn't bad for a whole building, but it was way more
than I could dream of getting together. You had to bring
twenty percent with you in cash to even be allowed to
bid. Crazy. And it was way more than that, really, because it said property bought at auction had to be up to
code in a year or the city could take it back. That would
cost a fortune! New plumbing, new wiring, insulation,
and lights over stairs—all kinds of things. Hopeless.
We were going to lose it, unless no one bought it.
Could we disrupt the auction, or make the building
look so bad no one would want it? There had to be
something we could do, but when I thought of telling
Skip and Lorenzo and Eddie, I realized I didn't have
much faith in them. Lorenzo would just move out. Skip

would panic. Eddie would go to sleep. I needed Mitch.

I jumped up to get my sketchbook. Mitch hadn't left an address, but I was sure I knew where he was.

I flipped to a blank page and once I started writing, I went on and on. I had months of things to tell him in addition to everything I should have said when he was still here. When I'd filled up three pages I put them in an envelope and addressed it to Mitch Mahoney, General Delivery, Brooklin, Maine. I didn't know the zip code so I added an extra stamp. The post office could look it up. I didn't put a return address because I didn't want it back. I looked at my watch and saw it was after eleven. Stumps still hadn't shown up, and while I knew I wasn't supposed to leave the house empty, I also wasn't supposed to be left here all alone. So I broke the rule and ran out in the rain to the mailbox on Broadway and jogged all the way back. I knew that it was about as rational as writing to Santa at the North Pole, but I felt easier after I'd sent it. I felt like I could sleep. I shoved the auction book deep into my backpack to hide it. I had delegated the question of what to do to a higher authority, and now I could rest.

The sound of the door opening and closing woke me but no one came upstairs. It was drizzling off and on again; maybe I'd just heard wind or rain.

"Hello?" I called from the top of the stairs. Street light filtered in from the round window over the door. Someone was slumped there.

"Siiiid," Stumps moaned.

I rushed down. His forehead was bleeding.

"Got jumped," he said.

"Let me help you!"

He gasped while trying to stand. "I fell on my knee."

"How could you get mugged? You look like you're collecting cans!" He had a wool cap pulled to his eyebrows and he'd been carrying his stuff in a garbage bag.

"They didn't want my stuff." Stumps held onto me, and we went slowly up the stairs. "I think it was those guys from the deli. Shit, that burns." He looked at his hand. It was scraped up where he'd fallen on it. "You got any meds? Percocet?"

"The guys from the deli? What'd they say?"

"Said we gotta get lost, yo."

I helped Stumps onto the couch upstairs and peeked out the window.

"They're in a van, you see it?"

"Yeah." It was idling at the end of the block. "If only we had a way to call the cops."

"They're here too," Stumps said. He flexed his knee a little, wincing.

It was true. Down by Broadway. A patrol car.

"Dude said," Stumps breathed hard, maybe in pain or trying to hide his fear, "if we know what's good for us, we scramble before the cops go off duty. They said, *Go inside, tell your little pals, get your stuff, and clear out.*"

"Shit!" I found a clean T-shirt in my bag and managed to wrap it around Stumps's head. I had some Tylenol in my backpack.

"No vodka?"

"We're getting out of here." I looked around. We had so much stuff, I didn't know what to take.

"That's what I was thinking. Except I don't want to go out there."

"We have to go. No one else is here. We have to call around, tell everyone what happened, not to come, they could get hurt."

I rushed around looking for my flashlight. I bundled my bed into a lump. I remembered that someone had left a laundry cart downstairs. I raced back down the dark stairs for it. There was so much I couldn't take. Tools. Clothes. Upstairs—everyone's sleeping bags.

"Listen, if we take a bunch of stuff and go quickly, they shouldn't mess with us, right? It'll look like we're scared . . ."

"Look like?" He attempted to laugh.

"We'll take a bunch of stuff, we'll look like no threat. Then they think it's over and they won and no one comes back for a few days and they'll be less vigilant. Let's go while the cops are here."

We got ourselves arranged in the foyer. Stumps could barely walk, his knee must have been swelling up, but there was no time to look at it. I had my backpack on and a laundry cart full of stuff. Someone had left a bicycle with two flat tires. "Here, use this like a walker,"

I said. Stumps held it while I tied a bundle to the rack on the back wheel.

When I was done, we looked at each other, and Stumps flashed his gold tooth at me in an attempt at a smile. "Where we going, Squids?" he asked.

"My house." I unlocked the door. The rain had picked up.

We lurched out with our awkward packs. Water dripped in my eyes while I locked the door behind me. I hadn't thought to find an umbrella and I wasn't going back inside now. We stepped onto the sidewalk and headed north.

"Keep your head down," I said to Stumps when we passed the van.

Another block. A car approached and my stomach turned, but it was just a town car. Shit, it could have been a car service. I didn't think to flag it down until it was gone.

"Should we call a car?" I asked. But I wouldn't know how to find a quarter in this crazy bag.

"How? We can't stand around and wait." Stumps was struggling with the bike.

"You got that?" It was heavy with the stuff on back and hard to push. But so was the stupid flimsy laundry cart.

"Just keep moving," he said.

"Are they following us?"

"Don't look."

We passed the pay phone in front of a shuttered

hardware store. It was the phone I'd called my dad from the other day. I had a flash of longing to call him now; like when I'd gotten in a fight with a boy in fifth grade and called him crying from the nurse's office because I had a cut over my eye. He came to pick me up in his truck and took me out for ice cream—and suddenly it hadn't seemed so bad anymore. We'd even laughed about it.

Wheels cut through the wet street, moving slowly. Stumps stiffened beside me, twisted his head to look back. "Shit," he said, and I spun around.

It was a van. We started hurrying toward an awning. "Should we turn?" I asked.

The van passed. *Goldsmith Butchers*, the side read. The driver peered out at us curiously and passed, splashing through puddles.

"Damn," Stumps grimaced.

I'd barely noticed the slope up to Grand Avenue before. It was probably only two miles to the Bakery. I was sweating in my layers but if I took anything off, the heavy pack that was jabbing my spine would be worse. What the hell was that? A book? A screwdriver?

"Hey, Boston Bruiser around at your house?" Stumps panted.

"Who, Mitch?"

"That his name? I met him at Rot-Squat?"

"He moved to Maine."

"Oh. I liked that dude. Tough guy. No bullshit."

It was too painful to think of Mitch and my stupid desperate letter and the angry way he had left the Bakery. I didn't try to answer. A movement made us both start. A ragged mutt, no collar, skittered around the corner. It saw us and froze, head down. Then it skulked sideways into the street, like it was afraid. Of us. It was almost funny. The dog and I watched each other with wary eyes until we turned onto Grand. I felt safer here where there were more cars and lights, even an open deli. Two more blocks. One more block.

Finally, our corner. The fading letters in the bricks over the door—*Sunshine Crust Baking Factory*. The familiar painted rays of flaking orange. The bolt turned and we were out of the rain.

XVI

Lee and a vanload of his friends from the city came to the Bakery the next afternoon. After getting Stumps settled in Raven's bed the night before, I'd spent an hour getting soaked at the pay phone on the corner, getting ahold of everyone I could and telling them what happened. Lee and his friends had baseball bats with them. They marched up the stairs, bristling with testosterone, like a posse in a Western. Stumps had finally woken up after sleeping for twelve hours. He was propped against the wall under Raven's loft working on the veggie burger Abby had gotten him at Kellogg's Diner. He had a bag of peas on his swollen knee. His belongings, still soaked from our crazy walk, were spread all over the kitchen to dry. He crammed the rest of his french fries into his mouth and got up to join Lee, wincing when he put weight on his leg.

Abby was pissed. "You're messed up, you have to stay put!" She looked like a little girl in her skirt and pigtails, especially with all the tall men in the room.

"I'm just going to identify the dudes," Stumps told her. "I won't get out of the van, I promise."

"We can't just let this go," Lee growled. "We're not

going to forfeit the building to a bunch of thugs."

Abby turned on him. "You're fucking crazy. This is bullshit."

"This isn't Lee's fault, Abs." Stumps leaned on the loft, looking pale.

"It's not exactly *not* his fault."

Lee's friends ignored her and started filing back downstairs. It seemed like a terrible idea to me too, though I was glad they were going to try to get our tools and things out.

Stumps gave me a high five and said, "Good times, Squids."

When Lee passed me I said, "I'm sorry, I know I should come along, I'm just . . ."

"No worries," he replied. "You did enough last night."

"Why are you apologizing to this asshole?" Abby yelled. "Get the fuck out of our house!" She threw herself in a kitchen chair and rubbed her eyes. "I hope those idiots get their asses kicked."

I sat down with her. "Where's Raven?"

"In the city, I guess."

I wanted to tell Abby about the auction, but I couldn't bring myself to mention it. My throat hurt. I was tired. It all seemed too hard.

Soon there were steps on the stairs. "What was all that shouting?" Skip asked. "Who were those guys?"

"Oh shit," I said, "did you lock the door behind them?"

"I did. What's going on, all these people in and out?"

"Jesus!" Abby got up. "What are you, her mom?"

"I just—"

Abby slammed the door of her room behind her.

Skip chewed his lip and waited. I put my head in my arms on the table. There was no way I could deal with him right now. He headed back downstairs.

I went into my room and got back in bed. I took the auction book out of my backpack and looked at it again. The picture was still there. Our address, in black-and-white. I studied the numbers until they blurred, hoping I was seeing them wrong and it was someone else's house in the book. I hid the booklet under my mattress and shut my eyes. Falling asleep, I felt it glowing beneath me, turning my bed into a magic carpet, floating me terrifyingly away from the Bakery. I clutched the bed as if I would fall off, into a void.

I know how much you care about this house. Fragments of my letter to Mitch came back to me on the subway the next morning. I felt awful, but I'd called in sick yesterday—I had to show up today. My coffee tasted bad. I couldn't drink it. I couldn't read. I just stared glassy-eyed at the ground while words from the letter spun in my head like a mantra. *I know how much you care about this house.* I tried to imagine how that would sound when he read it. *If* he read it.

I made it to work and propped myself up at the desk. I wondered how bad it would look if I put my head down and shut my eyes. It seemed like a really good idea.

Kathy clicked down the hallway and asked, "Sid, did the mail come yet?" and I tried to sit up straight. The sharpness of her voice made me wince. Everything was painful, her heels on the floor, the red of her nails.

"Are you all right? You're very flushed." The sweetness of her cool hand on my forehead brought tears to my eyes. I had to bite my lip to keep them back. "You've got a fever. You shouldn't have come in," Kathy said firmly. She gave me a twenty and said to take a cab home and pick up soup and Tylenol on my way. I couldn't even thank her, I only nodded. Her kindness was making it worse. I felt tears coming on in a big way and I had to get home before the storm broke.

I had trouble making my key work at the Bakery; it wouldn't turn. You always had to wiggle it just so and it took some strength to twist the long bolt Mitch had rigged and I was so weak. I finally got it open, and that was it. I couldn't do anything more, so I simply sat down inside.

"Why's the door open?"

I blinked and Skip was there above me, his hair swinging down over his face.

"Oh my god, are you okay?"

I seemed to be sprawled on the floor, my limbs so heavy I could barely move. How long had I been here? My messenger bag was right there next to me.

"You're burning up!" Skip's hand felt just like Kathy's. "I'm going to help you upstairs," he said as he placed an arm under my shoulder.

I managed to stand but the room spun and I leaned back against the wall, clutching his arm. "I'm sorry," I said, and tears spilled down my jacket. "I'm so sorry."

"You're just sick. Come on."

We struggled up the narrow stairs. I couldn't see because my eyes were wet and I was dizzy, and when we got to the second floor and my mural, I completely broke down. Why had I never finished it? Why had I been unable to see what I had until it was slipping away?

"I'm so sorry." I held onto Skip. "You were right, and now it's too late . . ."

Eddie was on my other side now and the next stairs were easier. Skip said, "You'll finish it, don't worry." But he didn't know. I hadn't told them about the auction.

Finally, I was in bed and Skip put the Tylenol in my hand. Eddie held a jug of water. I tried to tell them, but I wasn't making sense, they wouldn't listen.

"Later," they said. "Rest."

I blinked away a dream like I was fighting my way up out of deep water. Skip was crouching over my bed. It was light out, morning.

"You've got to stop apologizing," he said. "It's me who should apologize. I shouldn't have flown off the handle like that."

I couldn't breathe, my head was so stuffed up, from being sick or from crying, I couldn't tell. I pushed the pillows against the wall and tried to prop myself up higher. My boots were off and I was under my quilt in my jeans. When I moved, everything hurt. Needles shot through my head. Skip handed me a napkin from the deli and I blew my nose.

"But I should have talked to you," I said. My voice was nasal and thick. "About them staying and all that. I put you in a bad position." I saw that Lorenzo was in my room too, slouched in my easy chair with an ankle resting on his knee.

Skip nodded and chewed his lip like he didn't know what to say. Finally he asked, "You feeling any better?"

"You've been so nice," I said, choking up. When everyone was rude I could be stoic and tough, but their kindness destroyed me.

"I called my aunt who's a nurse," Skip said. "She told me you need to have lots of liquids and rest." He pulled an orange juice carton out of a bag and set it in front of me like an offering. Then he looked at Lorenzo.

"I brung you a tape," Lorenzo shrugged, comically. He reached to hand it to me. "We made a demo."

I took it and looked at it without really seeing it. I was flattered that Lorenzo wanted me to have it. But then, in another way, it kind of made me embarrassed for him. This was what he brought to a sick person? It was so . . . self-absorbed.

"That's cool," I said. "Thanks."

"Don't matter now." Lorenzo sank lower in the chair. "Fuckin' Elio quit."

"Your drummer? He was so good!"

"Yeah. He got that stupid emo band with that

straight-edge ass-wipe. We coulda opened for Neurosis! But he got some show he don't wanna cancel and fuck that. We say us or them, man." Lorenzo chewed on a dreadlock. "Now Timmy don't wanna do nothing either."

"You can start a new band—"

"I got some friends in Mexico City wanna do stuff," he shrugged again. "Be good to be there for the winter anyway."

After they left, I studied the cassette: a badly photocopied image of some kind of carnage, six songs. He'd come to New York to do something and here it was—six songs. Now he was done.

"Sid." Skip's nervous voice woke me. "Where's the light?"

I fumbled for the lamp over my bed. I thought I must still be asleep and confused, because as my eyes adjusted to the glow I saw my father, wearing an unlikely suit jacket, standing in the doorway with Skip. He looked so strange in my little room against the walls I had painted bright red, my Crass posters and books and records, the velvet chair I'd found on the street, the familiar pile of laundry taking over the floor.

"Dad! I was supposed to meet you!" I tried to sit up but my head spun.

"It's okay." He sat down on my bed. "You didn't answer your beeper so I came to find you."

"How'd you . . . ?"

"Well, I write to you here, don't I?" He smiled. "I got a map."

"I'm sick."

"I can see that. It sounds like your friend Skip here's taking good care of you." We both looked up at Skip who hovered in the doorway. "I'll get you groceries and stuff. Tell me what else you need. Do you need to see a doctor?"

"Where's Angela?"

"We're just here for the night so she went ahead to the thing."

"You're missing it."

"It doesn't matter. And I can stay longer if you need me to. Angela could take the train back or—"

"I'm okay. I just need to rest. I don't have a fever anymore. I'm just really tired."

My dad looked around again. He saw my teddy bear sitting on the trunk by my bed and picked him up. "Ol' Woozy is still around, look at that. He looks right at home in here. Should I let you sleep?"

"No, now you're here, talk to me." I snuggled back down in my bed. "What else is going on?"

"Oh, get this. I got a wacky letter from your mother last week."

"Oh no." My mom used to write a lot when I was a kid, self-pitying scrawls that scared me. My dad made me write back but I couldn't tell her anything real, she was too fragile.

"Have you been in touch with her?" my dad asked.

I shook my head, guilty. I hadn't talked to my mom since I'd run away from her house in New Hampshire three years ago, when her new babies and new husband and new life made me feel so angry and invisible and bad.

"So, listen to this. She tells me that a young man from Brooklyn, who she identified as your *boyfriend*, appeared to her at her place of work. Like a sighting of the Virgin Mary."

My heart pounded. I tried to sit up higher. "Who? What?"

"Well, I hoped *you* would enlighten *me*!" My dad laughed like it was a great joke, and Skip laughed with him. "You got a boyfriend you keeping secret?"

"Did she tell you a name?" I asked. But I knew it was Mitch. I had told him that my mom worked at Home Depot in Portsmouth. If he was in Maine, like I thought, he was close by.

"You got so many boyfriends now, you don't know which one it could be, huh?" My dad and Skip laughed some more. "Well, your mom's a little loopy but she seemed to take it as a sign. Like you wanted to be in touch with her. Maybe you could send her a card or something, now that she's gotten her hopes up."

He gave me a worried smile I knew well. Worry for my mom, for me. He expected me to tell him she could go to hell, and then he'd wince with pain for me, blaming himself. But what my mom had seen as a hopeful sign was the sign I'd been waiting for too. The sign from Mitch.

"I will," I said. My dad looked at me strangely. I noticed I was now gripping my old teddy bear so tight my knuckles were white. I released it, released my breath, and smiled. I felt happy. I felt hope. "I'll write to her."

Eddie came to check on me the next day. He brought chicken soup from Kellogg's and when I tried to explain I was a vegetarian, he laughed and said it was just *chicken* like I was still delirious. So I drank it anyway and he told me uplifting stories about people at AA, saying their names like I knew them all personally.

Skip brought water and juice and took my temperature again. He couldn't stop talking about how cool my dad was, how he couldn't believe he'd come to the squat and was fine with it all. Skip was in and out of my room so much that when Raven stopped by in the late afternoon, in a funny way it now seemed like she was the one who didn't belong.

"Can I visit you now?" She fidgeted in the doorway. "Skip wouldn't let me in yesterday, he said you had to rest."

"He's my nurse, I guess." I smiled at her. "God, what day is it?"

"Monday." She sat on my bed.

"Where have Jimmy and Abby been?"

"They went to Ohio. They're getting that car."

"What happened at the Theater?"

"Oh. God. Well, Lee and them didn't find anyone to beat up. They got the tools and stuff out. There's some stuff of yours out there." She gestured at the kitchen.

"That's good."

"No one's staying there. They're all talking big about how they'll go back, but . . ." She shrugged and stopped talking.

"Where've you been?" I asked.

"We had the hearing this morning so I was staying in the city."

I'd forgotten about the hearing. That was why Raven looked haggard again, like before she'd moved to Brooklyn. "How'd it go?"

Raven hugged her knees to her chest. "I don't know. We just made all these statements about what had happened and the judge listened and then she said there'd be another hearing in three months, and that was it."

"Three months? That's so long!"

"Our lawyer said it was normal, it went fine. I guess I thought it'd be more like in the movies." Now she started speaking in a big rush: "Sid, I have to get out of town. New York and this court case, it's making me crazy, and Veronica told me how this place is getting auctioned off and I can get a ride as far as Richmond if I go tonight, and I have to—I just have to go."

I nodded at her mutely.

"I'm so sorry." She threw herself down next to me and rubbed her shaggy head against my shoulder. "I feel like a bad friend, but I can't face another eviction."

"Don't feel bad. I understand."

"Being in court was so sucky. I kept thinking about

Rot-Squat and my room there and my friends and my life, and now it's this arguing about how many dollars our stuff was worth, like it makes any difference at all and if I stay in New York another second I'm going to kill someone."

"Where will you go?"

"These guys I know, their friends' band is leaving on tour and they need a driver. I can sell merch and stuff. Maybe I could focus on taking pictures again if I was traveling."

I put my hand on Raven's arm and squeezed. I felt the shadow of the tattoos banding her skinny arm, like my fingers could memorize them before she left. We breathed in sympathy and the breeze came in my window and washed over us and the highway purred beyond the trees. When she packed her backpack and left, I slept.

I slept the next day too. When I got up, I'd have to tell everyone about the auction, I'd have to figure out what to do, I'd have to start packing my stuff. I wanted to put it off a little longer. But the next afternoon I got up to use my piss bucket and realized I felt pretty good. My head was clear; I didn't ache. I heated water on the hot plate and gave myself a sponge bath. Then I walked around the house to stretch my legs. No one was home on my floor or downstairs. It was nice down on the second floor, with the autumn sun burning through the windows on the west and south walls so the room was golden and warm. I looked at my blurry unfinished mural in the rays of light. I didn't want to leave it like that, it wasn't right.

I ate a bagel from the food my dad had left. Then I found my work pants in the bottom of the laundry pile on my floor, and when I tugged them out, I saw the Green Day CD where it had rolled under my chair months ago.

I put the CD in Skip's boom box. The sun and the music were so good together, they gave me energy. The first paint can I opened was leftover red from my bedroom, so I started on the bricks in the wall Humpty Dumpty was sitting on. After a while, I stepped back to look. The red popped, it was cheerful. This was going to be cool. I had the music up high, so I didn't hear the front door, or steps on the stairs. I just looked up when familiar red-and-black Nikes came into view. I froze, kneeling on the floor, paint brush midair.

"Whatcha doin'?" Mitch asked. His hair was shaggier. It softened his features. His arms and face were very tan.

"I want to finish this," I answered, and somehow my voice sounded as calm as his.

He nodded, then put down his backpack and looked at the wall. "Lemme help."

It was easiest to follow his lead and act like he had only been gone an hour instead of six months. It gave me a chance to collect myself. I'd been half expecting him, but now that he was here, it wasn't the relief I'd expected. I felt short of breath, self-conscious, agitated.

He looked so different . . . I felt like I didn't know him at all and I was embarrassed now at the liberty I'd taken, writing to him like we were close, telling him I knew how he felt.

My hand trembled when I handed him a brush, but if he noticed, he didn't say anything. "I was going to use that blue for the sky," I said.

He opened the can neatly with my screwdriver and stirred. He started filling in the background around Humpty Dumpty's head. The brush I'd given him was small and there was a daintiness to his painting that seemed wrong for him; but he didn't complain, he kept going in a soothing, sweeping rhythm.

"This is a good blue," he said.

"It is."

"What'd you call it, royal?"

"It's more teal, I think. Maybe peacock." Now that he wasn't looking at me in my crusty old jeans, the bandanna over my hair, I was more comfortable. I could talk.

"Did you visit my mom?" I asked.

His hand stalled for a second. "She told you?"

"Actually, I'm not in touch with her."

"Yeah. I kind of figured that out."

"It's okay. I didn't tell you, how could you know?" I gave up trying to paint. It was too mesmerizing to watch Mitch, his broad shoulders stretching against the soft gray of his T-shirt. "She told my dad about it." Mitch was obviously embarrassed, which made me feel more in control. I smiled. "She decided you must be my boyfriend."

"I didn't say that," he mumbled.

"My mom's nuts."

He kept painting, blue sky stretching up and up. "She was nice, actually."

"Really?" I couldn't picture how she would be; I didn't know her well enough. "How did you, like, recognize her?"

He shot me a glance. "You kidding? She looks just like you. You have the same eyes."

"We do? What was she like?"

He smiled at the wall. "She got so excited when I said I knew you. She started asking me a million questions."

"Oh god, I'm sorry."

"Nah, it was sweet," Mitch said. "I'm the idiot who didn't know what he was getting into. I was just all casual, like, *Buying paint*, *saying hi*, and she got all, like . . . emotional. Her buddy there made her take a break and we got coffee."

"You went out for coffee with my mom?"

"She wanted to hear about you."

"What did you tell her?"

"I don't know. You know. I guess she talked more."

"Oh god," I said again. But he looked steady, still painting. He was here. It hadn't scared him off.

The CD ended and I looked at the boom box. The late-afternoon sun bounced off the metal in bright sparks.

"How was Maine?"

"Great!" Mitch answered.

It would be dark soon; the nights were getting chilly and I thought about shutting the window I'd opened, but I didn't get up.

Then he added, quieter, "And lonely. It was harder than I thought. I guess that's why I did weird shit like visit people's moms."

He shot me a shy smile that sent a wave of electricity through my bones.

"I got your letter," he said. And that was why he was here. He was wearing familiar-looking Levi's and the same beat-up sneakers. Why did he seem so different? I hadn't remembered him being so attractive. When I didn't say anything, he added, "About the auction?"

"I didn't tell anyone yet."

"You didn't? What, here in the house you mean?"

"No." I bit my lip. "Skip and Lorenzo and Eddie don't know. I was just so upset and I wrote to you, and then the other place we were squatting got fucked up and I got sick and . . . oh god." I put my head in my hands. "What are we going to do?"

Mitch crouched down next to me so I had to look right at him. "I don't know," he said, "but I like it when you say *we*."

I only had to lean forward to kiss him.

When everyone else got home, we'd tell them about the auction. We'd make a plan. But for now, thank god they were out. Mitch told me he knew he'd been a condescending jerk. He didn't want to live alone in the woods anymore. He kissed my forehead and my ears and the bandanna fell from my hair onto the floor and he whispered, "You're the toughest girl I ever met." It sounded so sweet and true, and suddenly I wasn't afraid of anything. We would lose this house very soon. But it would be okay. We were young and strong. We were just getting started.

Acknowledgments

Many thanks to my teachers Mermer Blakeslee and Tom Jenks; to Aaron Petrovich, Johanna Ingalls, and Johnny Temple at Akashic Books; and to my generous and clever readers, especially Sally Wolfe, Zachary Lipez, and Nick Forte. Also thanks to Kyanne Breden, Merilyn Wakefield, Amber Thalmayer, Art Hanlon, Lisa Marfleet, Jesse Pearson, Ash Thayer, Letha Rodman Melchior, Abigail Czapsky, and my comrades in the West Kortright Centre fiction workshop.